"Braly has a way of writing that makes you want to read everything he writes." *Kansas City Star*

"[Braly] thinks honestly about people, and writes about them with an unstressed absolute realism." Anthony Boucher

FELONY TANK

"A masterfully written novel... an ace work of noir fiction." Brian Greene, *CriminalElement.com*

ON THE YARD

"The characters in this book are at times shockingly inhuman and perverted, but always genuine." *San Francisco Chronicle*

"Uncompromising, grim and brutally frank." *Los Angeles Times*

MALCOLM BRALY BIBLIOGRAPHY

Felony Tank (1961)

Shake Him Till He Rattles (1963)

It's Cold Out There (1966)

On the Yard (1967)

The Master (novelization of the film Lady Ice, 1973)

False Starts: A Memoir of San Quentin
and Other Prisons (1976)

The Protector (novelization of the film, 1979)

FELONY TANK
BY MALCOLM BRALY

Black Gat Books • Eureka California

FELONY TANK

Published by Black Gat Books
A division of Stark House Press
1315 H Street
Eureka, CA 95501, USA
griffinskye3@sbcglobal.net
www.starkhousepress.com

Originally published in a slightly expurgated version
by Gold Medal Books, Greenwich, CT and copyright
© 1961 by Malcolm Braly. Reprinted by Tower
Publications, Inc, New York, date unknown.
Reprinted in an unexpurgated edition by Pocket
Books, New York, and copyright © 1976 by Malcolm
Braly.

ISBN: 1-933586-91-5
ISBN-13: 978-1-933586-91-5

Book design by Mark Shepard, shepgraphics.com

First Black Gat Edition: February 2016

FELONY TANK
BY MALCOLM BRALY

To Judy

PART ONE

CHAPTER ONE

Doug stepped off the bus broke and hungry. His last cash had dwindled on the trip across the desert, and when his ticket ran out in the drab southwestern city of Ardilla he couldn't even remember why he'd wanted to come here. It was night when the bus pulled in and the city seemed strange, stunted and dirty. In the depot where people were meeting each other, there was no one to meet him. No one to know he was here or worry if he wasn't.

He walked around a couple embracing and found his own face in the mirror of a cigarette machine. His hair was messed, rumpled from sleeping curled in the bus seat. Automatically he reached for his comb, but found he'd lost it. He was always losing combs. He'd never realized how hard it was to keep going from one day to the next. Though he now admitted his old man had kept things pieced together somehow, he still couldn't find any warmth in his memories of him. Even broke and hungry he was glad to be away.

There was nothing to do in the depot. His luggage was in his pockets, and he didn't have as much as a dime to put in the popcorn machine. He stared at an Indian woman in a beaded dress until she caught him, and, blushing, he hurried out.

The wind hit and he paused in the shelter of the doorway to turn his collar up. A newspaper rack was chained to an eyebolt set in the wall. He tried to pull it lose, but it was solid. There was probably a couple of dollars in dimes in the rack, but with the glass doors behind him and the blue of the depot neon lighting the pavement, there was no way he could get it.

He put his hands into his pockets, hunching against the cold, and the wind whipped his hair over his eyes. He was seventeen years old, tall, but still half-formed. Dressed in cords, run-over white shoes, two sweaters and a lumberman's jacket. The cords were the same ones he'd been wearing the day he didn't go home from high school. Instead he'd sailed his books one by one into Sullivan's Gorge and walked out to the highway. A week later he found a job in southern Oregon setting chokers for a logging crew. The first day he knew the job was too much for him, and they knew it too, but they let him work a week. He left in the night, taking besides his wages a hunting knife, a jacket, and a pair of boots.

The boots were too small and by the time he reached Sacramento, California, his toenails were turning purple and beginning to come loose. For the boots, and two bits extra, he'd bought the white shoes in a Goodwill Store.

In all the time since he'd run off, he hadn't known anyone to talk to who hadn't called him "kid."

Once, before he became so roadworn, he'd gone to a dance hoping to pick up a girl. His dancing was barely passable, and he'd stood around for an hour, patting his foot to the music, trying to work up his nerve. Finally he asked a girl who hadn't been on the floor twice the whole evening. She turned him down.

He was so embarrassed his hands felt swollen. As he started away he heard a girl laugh and he was sure it was at him. He found himself on the street wondering bitterly if he were funny looking. But he knew it wasn't that. He was too goddam young. He ran until he couldn't hear the music anymore.

After that he saw the suggestion of laughter in every girl's face, and he couldn't work up guts enough to even smile at them.

The wind blew an empty cigarette package into the doorway. It whirled and settled with a scratching sound. Doug heard the door open. A thick man in a big hat stopped beside him, and looked both ways on the sidewalk. His face was heavy and placid. Doug was beginning to move away when he heard:

"You live around town, son?"

He turned back uneasily. This couldn't be anything good.

"Yes," he lied. His voice surprised him by sounding calm.

The man settled his coat. "Pretty nippy," he announced, and then as if it were part of the same thought he went on: "I guess you probably still live with your folks?"

"Yes—sir." Doug's anxiety betrayed him into adding the "sir." He'd almost made up his mind the man was a cop, not a queer. The last time a cop had stopped him, he'd spent three days in a juvenile hall.

"They going to pick you up?"

"Oh, no—no, I guess I'll walk home."

He hated standing here, bobbing his head like a puppet, just because someone wanted to mind his business. The cop—he was sure now—turned and looked him full in the face. Doug could see the whites of his eyes in the shadow of his hat brim, but he couldn't read their expression.

"I did see you get off the bus, didn't I?"

When Doug nodded, the cop made a humorous noise and pointed with his toe at Doug's shoes. "Ain't many boys in this town wearing white shoes."

"We're new here. We're from California."

The cop chuckled. "Wouldn't hurt you none if you kept that a secret. Meanwhile, if you ever get caught downtown and can't get home, the Mission is two blocks down this way." He pointed to the left. "They'll fix you up for the night, and give you a chance to earn some breakfast. It's a big white place."

The cop paused, watching him carefully, and Doug nodded again and said, "I'll remember."

He knew enough to start in the direction pointed out to him, past a darkened barber shop and a men's store featuring a window display of Stetson hats. He looked back at the first cross street, but the cop was standing in the middle of the sidewalk still watching him.

He had to go up on the porch of the Mission, and while he was waiting he read the card under the night light.

These things I command you,
that ye love one another

John 15:17

*Ring this bell any hour
of the day or night.*

Doug didn't feel any impulse to push the bell. He didn't want to be taken care of. It burnt him that even a cop took one look and immediately started trying to tuck him into bed.

After a moment he peered around the edge of the building, and the sidewalk was clear.

Half an hour later he stood in the shadow of a billboard watching a small feed store. It stood a little apart from the other buildings on the block, and its rear was exposed in a dark alley.

He ran quickly across the street and into the alley. He dropped beside a garbage can, full of excitement.

In the back of the feed store he saw the dark sheen of glass. No bars. He was in luck.

The only bad moment was after he'd put the rock through the window. It made a booming crack, and some of the glass fell outward and rattled on the pavement. He threw his jacket over the broken glass still caught in the frame, and levered himself through the window, his feet scrabbling on the smooth wood.

Somewhere in the city chimes began to strike. It was just a little over an hour since he'd stepped off the bus.

CHAPTER TWO

The prowl car braked suddenly and fishtailed to a stop. Its siren groaned out. A long truck-and-trailer rolled by on the cross street. Huey swore bitterly.

"Goddam nitwits."

They'd been chasing a speeding hotrod all the way in from the city limits, but the little car had stayed ahead of them easily, cutting corners square and close, and at the last moment scooting around the front of the approaching truck. Pete had almost flipped the prowl car to avoid a collision.

When the truck had passed, the street ahead of them was empty. Those kids were probably blocks away by now, and that made Huey salty because he knew they were laughing at him.

"Circle," he told Pete. "Maybe we can pick them up."

Huey was a hunter, manhunter as it happened, but that was just an accident of time and place. Under other circumstances he would have hunted other things.

Pete wound the car through the surrounding blocks as Huey watched for the cut-down shape of the hotrod. He was a big man, dressed in the regulation deputy's uniform except for high-heeled boots, which put him well over six-four. He was only twenty-five, but his mixture of sternness and anger made him seem much older.

The streets were empty except for casual cars, and each time they turned into another quiet block Huey felt a fresh thrust of anger.

"Try some alleys," he directed. "Maybe they ducked in somewhere and turned their lights off."

He saw Pete shrug, and knew Pete would rather stop somewhere and have a cup of coffee. Well, that was too bad about him. If he didn't want to do his job he ought to get off the force.

The lights of the prowl car broke against the buildings and flooded along the alley walls.

In the second block, Huey saw something glittering on the black asphalt.

"Hold it!"

He switched on his swivel spotlight and picked up the broken glass in the circle of light. He grunted, and ran the spotlight up the side of the building. One window glared with reflected light, the other was empty except for bits of glass around the edge like irregularly spaced teeth.

Huey's impressions organized themselves automatically, and he told Pete to stand guard over the broken window. "We might have something in there," he said meaningfully.

He pulled the large flashlight out of its clamp above the windshield and stepped out of the car, drawing his revolver.

The lock on the front door of the feed store was a common type, and the second master key Huey tried opened it. He swore silently when the door creaked, but standing dead still, he heard a flurry of movement in the dark store.

Quickly he snapped the flash up in the direction of the noise, but it didn't cross anything except wooden bins and burlap bags, slumped half full.

"All right!" he shouted. "Stand up. You're boxed in!"

His hand was tense on the butt of his gun as he jerked the flashlight back and forth. But when he saw that his light wasn't going to draw fire, he stepped inside, his boot heels hitting sharply on the wooden floor.

"Come on," he said more reasonably. "You can't get out."

He paused, listening, but now there wasn't a sound. The air was heavy with the smell of chicken mash, and some darker odor suggesting earth. His light moved over coils of garden hose and the clean blades of new shovels, past a revolving rack of seed packets and the segmented stacks of flowerpots.

He figured the burglar must be crouching behind one of the counters. Switching the flash off, he tiptoed to the side, trying to work into a position from which he could see the whole store. He was still moving, testing his footing so the floor wouldn't creak, when he caught the blur of a moving figure out of the corner of his eye. He spun and snapped a shot over his shoulder, feeling a sudden chilling elation when the figure dropped.

The burglar had his head buried in his arms, but there was a tenseness in his huddled posture that caused Huey to stay on the alert. The man was conscious. With the toe of his boot Huey nudged him over, and when he saw the burglar's face he shook his head angrily. It was just a boy, his expression icy with shock, his eyes glittering in the harsh beam of the flashlight.

Huey dropped to one knee. "You hit, kid?"

The boy's throat worked and his mouth moved numbly for a moment. Then he said something.

"What?" Huey asked quietly.

"I don't know." It was just a whisper.

Huey ran his hand under the boy's jacket and felt carefully for blood, then checked his arms and legs. He's not hit, he concluded, getting to his feet. Just scared. And suddenly Huey was angry again. He'd missed. Score 97 on the range and miss a shot like that.

Steps sounded behind him, and Huey turned to see Pete in the doorway with his own gun drawn.

Huey roared at him. "I thought I told you to watch that window!"

Pete stepped inside. "I heard a shot."

"I don't care if you heard a goddam cannon!"

Pete ignored him and looked down at the boy. "Did you get him?" he asked.

"Nah. I shot to scare him. It's just a kid."

After Huey phoned the owner of the store, they took their prisoner directly to the county jail. In the prowl car Huey tried to question him, but the boy was still too shook up to talk—or he pretended to be. It was too dark to tell much about him, but Huey began to suspect that the kid's show of terror might be mostly put on, an act, to gain sympathy or to make them careless so he could try to run again.

The county courthouse sat like a square brick oven in a block of lawn and shrubbery. Huey saw a few lights in the county offices as the car circled around towards the back. The jail occupied the top two floors—floor and a half, really, since the felony section, built as a maximum security addition, was nothing but a bare concrete box sitting on the roof, five stories up and as isolated as the moon. When it was built, ten years before, the prisoners promptly named it the Penthouse.

Huey felt satisfaction whenever he looked up at the Penthouse. He knew that many regarded it as an eyesore, but the men it held secure had made nastier eyesores—killings and rape, cuttings and just plain beatings, robbery and all kinds of stealing—and when Huey caught someone he knew the felony tank would make sure they stayed caught.

The prowl car rolled down a concrete ramp and stopped in a large basement garage.

"Let's go," he told the kid.

The boy didn't move, and Huey caught sight of his face, half hidden in the shadowed back seat, closed in that quiet hostility that Huey found so irritating.

"Come on, move it!"

They took the elevator up to the booking office on the fourth floor, where the sergeant on duty turned out to be Al Haines. Al was levered back in a swivel chair looking like he hadn't moved for about six months, and he didn't get up when they came in.

"What you got?" he asked, yawning.

"Burglar," Huey answered tightly. He didn't like laxness. "Let's book him. We gotta get back on the road."

Turning towards the door that led out into the lower jail, Huey saw the sullen trusty they called Slim. He was leaning against the frame, scratching his cheek, taking everything in. Al usually had someone around to talk to, but Huey figured he could have picked almost anyone and done better. Slim was silent, leaden-eyed and obviously hostile. Lazy to boot.

Huey remembered him well. A man who should have gone to state prison for robbery, but somehow managed to get off with a county jail sentence. And it seemed like every time Huey came into the jail he saw Slim standing around with a broom in his hand—not that he was about to use it—and if you said anything to him he could squeeze a world of insolence into a simple yes or no. Huey promised himself that if he ever caught Slim around town he'd give him something substantial to sneer about—something like a broken leg.

"Looks like one for the juvenile tank." That was Al Haines, up off his tail and fumbling with the charge book.

"Maybe not," Huey said sharply. "We caught him inside. And he tried to run on me."

"Got a little rabbit blood, huh, kid?" Al asked. He wasn't looking for an answer.

Huey turned and deliberately studied the boy in the light to fix his face, along with a lot of others, in his memory.

The kid was bigger than he had seemed at first. Five-eleven maybe and he'd go about a hundred and sixty-five pounds. He didn't seem to be paying any attention to what they were doing to him. He stood hunched over the handcuffs, staring defiantly at the floor. Filthy cords and worn-out shoes. Those shoes had seen a lot of walking. He had about ten pounds of hair and it must have been months since it was cut. Road kid, Huey concluded. Stealing his way across the country. His mouth was young and his upper lip was just beginning to darken with fuzz, but there was something in the set of his brows that suggested maturity. A forced maturity, but still one that needed to be dealt with.

Huey gave his opinion. "I think we better lock him up tight."

"How old are you, kid?" Al asked.

The boy hesitated and rubbed his wrist so the chain on the handcuffs clinked softly.

"I'm eighteen."

Al shrugged. "Well, I guess he goes into the Penthouse." He studied the boy a moment longer, then advised, not unkindly, "You watch yourself up there, kid."

CHAPTER THREE

That was a fool thing to say, Doug told himself bitterly. He watched the cell door open and stop with a sharp "clang."

There wasn't a man in sight, but Doug could sense the congested life locked up all around him. He hesitated in front of the open door, but then he saw the jailer outside the tank motioning for him to shake it up. He took a deep breath and slipped into the cell. The door slammed shut behind him.

There were four bunks, two on each side, an upper and a lower. Three of them were full, the heavy figures muffled in their blankets, but the lower right was empty. Doug slipped into it, still holding his blanket roll. He wanted to get out of sight because he couldn't see how the men in the cell could still be asleep after the noise the door had made.

He thought he knew why he'd lied about his age. He was sick of being called "kid"—it was just another way for people to tell him they didn't think he was much of anything. Kid. Besides, he didn't want to go to another juvenile tank, where he'd be up to his neck in probation officers trying to find out where he lived, who his parents were and all the rest of it.

That was how he felt standing in the booking room. But when they'd taken him upstairs and he'd seen the cold gray metal of the felony tank and heard the cell door banging shut, he'd been scared. Like a little kid he had wanted to shout: *I take it back!*

He was still scared, huddled on the bare mattress. The cell seemed too quiet, as if it were waiting for something, and even though he couldn't see them, he was intensely conscious of the presence of the other three men. Somewhere out in the tank a small light made crazy shadows in the cell, and there was the whisper of heavy breathing. Somewhere a man groaned, and metal thudded with a soft hollowness.

As soon as he got over the worst of his nervousness, Doug realized he was cold, and he was thinking about unrolling his blankets when he heard a quiet voice directly above him.

"Hey—Agnes. We caught a fish."

Another voice answered sleepily from somewhere across the cell. "What?"

"Someone just came in."

"In here?"

Doug heard movement over his head and he lay perfectly still, feeling his heart against the mattress. The darkness of the bunk above him seemed to press against his face.

"Damned if they didn't. Hey, buddy...."

Doug hoped they would think he was asleep. He wasn't ready to talk or answer a lot of questions. But the voice persisted.

"Hey, you!"

He began to fake a loose snoring noise, and the quieter voice directly above him said, "Sounds like a wino."

"Damned if he don't. How'd you like to be gassed like that?"

"Yeah, but think how he's going to feel when he wakes up in jail."

"Where do you think you're going to wake up?"

"Sure, but at least I know it."

"Now that's a big help."

Both the voices seemed young and their speech was slurred with a western flavor that made them sound scoffing, but friendly. There was silence for a moment, and Doug was wondering if he could unfold his blankets without tipping them that he was awake, but then he heard:

"Hey, Billy. Want to roll him?"

There was a pause, and Doug forgot to snore. He hoped he'd be ready to fight if they tried to mess with him, but he couldn't be sure. He got scared at the wrong times.

The voice he'd identified as Billy said, "Maybe we better not. I didn't get a good look at him. He might turn out to be nine foot tall."

"If he is, we'll sic him on Carl. That'd be something to see."

One of them laughed softly.

They went on talking in whispers, and when Doug was sure they were no longer interested in him, he stopped making the snoring noise. He lay quietly listening. In the other lower bunk across from him, he could make out a grayish face, the mouth a slowly moving dark blur.

He was beginning to drift away into his own thoughts when the quality of whispering above him changed and took on the simmer of compressed emotion. He realized right away he had no business listening. But he listened anyway.

They were talking about something they must have talked about hundreds of times because there were big holes of silent understanding. Still the import was clear: escape.

How could they hope to? Doug had looked at the tank on the way in. Everything was barred and double-doored. But he could tell they were serious, because deep in their voices there was a note of constant anxiety.

They were waiting for something they needed—blades, they called them, and Doug immediately thought of knives. They expected someone named Slim to bring them.

That was all they really said, but they went on talking about whether he would bring them or whether he wouldn't—talking just because it was important to them, and the more they talked about it the more possible it seemed.

He was so cold he was beginning to shiver. Quietly he began to unfold his blankets. He was hungry for warmth and sleep, a chance to forget for awhile. He felt something slip in the blankets and grabbed for it, but he bumped it with the back of his hand. Whatever it was, it hit the floor with a sharp clatter. The silence was awful for him. It drew into the cell like a physical cold, making him feel empty and, somehow, wrong.

"That sonofabitch was on the Erie!"

"Maybe not—"

"I tell you, the sonofabitch was listening. Laying down there and taking everything in. Hey! Asshole!"

Doug couldn't move his mouth. What could he say? He knew he hadn't done anything but he felt guilty.

"All right," the voice went on grimly. "Play dead. We'll see about it in the morning."

"Easy, Agnes."

"Easy, my ass!"

A figure slipped out of the upper bunk. Doug rolled over against the wall. He didn't know whether he could fight or not.

A match flamed, and he saw a hard face staring at him. Two of them. Someone else was hanging over the top bunk. The man holding the match laughed. "A brat!"

The match went out, and the voice went on in the darkness. "Listen, kid, you better forget our business. If you've got any idea of living to get out of jail, you better dummy on *anything* you hear in this cell. You know what I mean?"

Doug felt his arm gripped in the darkness, gripped hard, and after a moment he realized that he was nodding his head when no one could see him. He managed to say, "Yes."

"Okay. And don't try anything sneaky. There isn't anything you can say in any part of this jail I won't hear about it before you can close your mouth. You hear?"

"Yes."

"You better."

They left him alone after that. He got under his blankets but he couldn't feel warm. He wanted to stand up to say you can trust me. I'd never snitch on anyone. But he knew how it'd be. They'd keep looking at him, wondering if he was going to tell. Making themselves angry thinking about it. And if anything went wrong they'd blame him, and probably try to kill him. He saw the hard face in the matchlight coming at him with a knife, and the flame of the match swelled up until he couldn't see anything

Sometime before he went to sleep, he remembered his wrist watch. He'd pushed it way up on his arm, and they hadn't found it when they shook him down. Now he slipped the watch off and put it in his pocket. He went to sleep dreaming of knives.

CHAPTER FOUR

Al came downstairs, back from locking up the fish. He racked the tank key beside the door and settled into his chair, sighing as if he'd done a day's work. Slim smiled to himself, a bitter, healing smile. Well now, he thought, another dangerous mission successfully completed.

Al looked vaguely worried, and Slim stared at him, waiting.

"What'd you think of him?" Al asked.

"He's a *real* bastard."

"What?"

"Huey. He's a bastard."

"No. I meant that kid. The one I just locked up."

Slim smiled slightly. "He's in serious trouble."

Al leaned forward. "He didn't look eighteen. Sixteen, maybe. But I don't see why he'd want to lie, do you?"

"Don't worry, he'll live through it."

Al said, "Hell, it might do him good."

Slim nodded in satirical agreement. It was no skin off his ass.

Al nodded back like a cartoon bear, round-eyed and simple, satisfied as long as someone seemed to agree with him. He sighed again and loosened his uniform belt.

Al started talking about his weight, how nothing seemed to help—as if anything would, the way he stuffed his face—and Slim nodded and said something in the intervals when Al stopped for assurance, but Slim wasn't really listening.

He nodded and stared at the scarred linoleum, breathing the tired stale smell of the jail and wishing he was out of it. But he didn't let himself go far thinking that way. He'd been in too many times, and he knew that the only way to stay sane was to think about the little bumps on each day—the tiny differences in routine that could grow to seem so important.

That led him to Agnes. It was a fool's setup and Slim wouldn't have given it headroom if it hadn't been for the cigarettes involved. Cigarettes were money and Slim always needed money. He played poker and lost.

That was the only reason he listened to Agnes, because to Slim, Agnes wasn't regular—he was a loudmouth hillbilly who wore his Levis too tight, and combed his hair like some punk movie star. Slim dismissed Agnes's partner Billy as a pimpled moon drifting around an Okie sun.

Agnes had scraped together a reputation for toughness, but he fought with his hands and Slim knew that no one was tough with a shiv in his belly. He'd seen a lot of the tough ones cut down and pounded into the pavement, while he—skinny and bitter—had endured.

Also Agnes was unseasoned. Slim was an old con, a veteran of his own peculiar war and fiercely proud of his service, and he didn't really trust anyone who hadn't served big time. So when Agnes had called him over to the bars while they were feeding the tank, Slim had been automatically untrusting.

But he listened, watching Agnes carefully out of his quiet gray eyes, and when he heard about the hacksaw blades he could hardly keep a straight face. What did this kid think he was going to do with hacksaw blades? Might as well try to cut down a tree with a pocket knife.

Slim knew the felony tank. He'd been in it for six months fighting his own case, and if he'd ever seen a tight can it was the Penthouse. Remote-control locking devices, automatic alarms, case-hardened steel—the whole works. Hacksaw blades would be worse than useless, because even if they could get through the tank bars, which wasn't likely, they still had the bars on the window to beat. No. It was impossible.

But all he'd said was, I'll see what I can do.

He was pretty sure he could get the blades, and Agnes had offered him three cartons of cigarettes, which was a fair price, but you didn't let a hoosier off with a fair price. Slim decided to hold off and see how much they would pay, and in making this decision he was conscious of a sense of power. They were locked up. Helpless. They couldn't make a move without him, and what they didn't know was that they couldn't make a move with him—not even with a boxcar full of hacksaw blades.

But he didn't intend to tell them that.

CHAPTER FIVE

Morning hit Doug all at once. The lights came on, the cell doors rolled and banged, toilets flushed, and a medley of voices grumbled and wisecracked.

"Come on, you sad bastards—"

"Dummy up!"

"Breakfast is served."

"Oh, dee-lightful!"

"*Chow!*"

Doug sat up. The cell door was open. Through two more sets of bars he saw a gray morning beginning to form outside the windows. A man passed, buttoning his pants. He was yawning and shaking his head.

Doug heard someone clearing his throat and turned to see a fat man sitting up in the lower bunk across from him. He was fully clothed except for his shoes. An older man, his face swollen with sleep.

"You come in last night?"

Doug nodded, uncomfortable because the man was staring at him, harder and longer than he should have, rubbing his mouth with a thick red hand. He was thick and heavy all over.

"You better get your breakfast. They don't serve it in bed."

The man started out of the cell, but paused in the doorway. "My name's Carl. You talk any?"

"Sure, I talk." Doug was going to say when I feel like it, but he didn't. He thought of a lot of things he couldn't quite say.

"I just wondered," Carl said, and left.

Doug stood up. His head was higher than the top bunks, and he couldn't help staring anxiously at the two men sleeping in them. He recognized the man he'd seen in the matchlight—

the one called Agnes. His face was to the side on the pillow of his arm, and his mouth moved a little with his even breathing. He seemed younger than he had the night before. Doug thought he looked like the younger brother of the good guy in a western movie; the one who was wild, but you knew he wasn't really bad. Even in his sleep Agnes seemed alert, as if he were waiting and hoping something would go wrong, because he knew he could handle it.

"He meant it."

Doug turned quickly into the aisle, taking a step back towards the door. The other one was sitting up, watching him. This one would be Billy. In a glance he knew Billy didn't scare him. Billy was skinny and pigeon-breasted, with a rotten complexion. Billy's eyes were pale gray, red-rimmed and crusted with sleep.

"I know he meant it," Doug said, "what's that s'posed to mean?"

"Just that you better watch yourself." Billy looked at Agnes as he said it, but Agnes didn't show any signs of waking up.

"You guys made your point. There's no sense in going on about it."

Billy looked a little uncertain. "I just wanted to make sure you understand."

Doug was satisfied with the way he had spoken up to Billy. He crossed his arms and looked at him deliberately. "Well, I understand all right."

Billy slid out of his bunk. He was wearing an old pair of striped shorts with one leg ripped nearly to the waist band. He had an angry scattering of pimples over his shoulders and back. Doug saw them as Billy bent to pick something up.

"If you're all right, you don't have to worry. Here's your cup. That must be what you dropped last night."

Doug accepted the metal cup, and after a momentary hesitation, he followed Billy out into the tank.

In the daylight it didn't seem big. About ten feet wide, maybe forty feet long. Doug looked around, made more curious by what he'd heard last night, and again he didn't see what they could do. The secret of the tank was simplicity. Three sides were bars, stretching from the floor to the ceiling; the forth side was closed off by the solid bulk of the cell block, a row of identical cages. Three feet beyond the bars there was a concrete wall, broken by narrow barred windows. In the corridor formed by the bars and the wall, two trustys in blue denim were pushing food through a long horizontal slot. A jailer in a green uniform stood a little apart, watching.

A knot of half-dressed men was crowded around the feeding slot, but they were standing quietly, waiting. One by one they headed away, carrying a bowl and a cup. They all seemed strange. One wore a little hat folded out of newspapers. Another had on what looked like a good suit, but he was shirtless, and the gray hair on his chest grew up around his neck like a sweater. A tiny bald man wore longjohns, and the trap had flopped half open, exposing his shriveled butt. Next was a young man in a gas-station outfit, complete except for the black leather tie. He even had a trade mark above his pocket, and that would have seemed silly to Doug except the man looked so scared.

Doug saw Billy talking to one of the trustys, and he recognized the trusty as the one who had been standing in the booking room the night before. A thin grayish man with a sharp eastern slant on his face. He was whispering to Billy, hardly moving his lips, and Billy looked worried. Doug was curious, but he looked away. He didn't want to know any more than he did already.

Doug was the last one served. One trusty dipped mush, three slices of bread on it, and shoved it at the slot. Doug took it and held his cup up to the bars for coffee.

He sat down on his own bunk and ate some bread. The oatmeal was in a metal bowl. Everything in the jail seemed to be metal. Even the toilet was metal and it stuck right out of the wall in plain sight.

"You say you come in last night?"

Doug met Carl's eyes and he didn't like them. They were too blue, too pressed with energy, and they looked strange in his tired red face. He needed a shave and his beard was like rust. A long time ago he must have been redheaded.

Doug answered because he didn't want everyone in the cell mad at him. "It was pretty late."

Carl said, "Must have been. I didn't hear a thing. You got a name?"

"Doug."

"Doug, huh?" Carl drank from his bowl like it was a cup. He didn't seem to pay any attention to what was in it. He shifted the bowl and held out his hand. "All right, Doug—"

Doug tried to make his shake firm, but Carl's hand was warm and moist, and he didn't let go right away.

Carl smiled, still squeezing. "You're just a youngster. What're you doing in here?"

"I'm old enough," Doug replied tightly, pulling his hand loose. He couldn't resist wiping his palm on his blanket.

Carl didn't miss the gesture. His smile turned into a grin, showing small yellow teeth. "Old enough for what?"

"Old enough to take care of myself."

"Kid, no one's that old."

Carl's shirt was the kind Doug thought of as a gambler's shirt. Green gabardine edged with solid white piping and the pockets were fastened down with little buttons like pills. In contrast, his jeans were faded and sun-bleached, rolled away from his bare feet. The toenails were broken and yellow and the skin seemed puffy around his ankles.

Doug drank some of the mush. It was barely sweetened, but milk had been mixed with it, enough to make it pour.

"Why don't we get spoons?" he asked Carl.

"Because they're afraid we'll cut each other's throats."

"With a spoon?"

"A spoon can be sharpened on the floor—" Carl slid his bare foot back and forth on the concrete—"until it goes in as easy as an ice pick. Sure as hell makes you just as dead." He grinned, then said, "They give us spoons at lunch and supper, but they count them and make sure they get them all back. If they don't, they turn off the TV. You think that don't produce spoons in a hurry?"

Doug finished his oatmeal and wiped the bowl with his bread. He was still hungry, but he was used to that. He tried the coffee. It was black, bitter without being strong. The cup was some kind of grayish soft metal, hotter than the coffee inside it.

He drank the coffee and listened to the noise of the tank: the wordless simmer of conversations, and running water. Somewhere someone was singing softly in Spanish, and someone else was swearing with a countrified exuberance. The air seemed dense, heavy with a complex of smells, all unpleasant: disinfectant, sweat, souring clothes and urine.

Well, you asked for it, didn't you? He wanted to feel equal to anything that could happen, but he knew in blunt truth he wasn't. The tank was too barren, emptier even than the gas station, bus depots and other featureless public places he had eaten and washed in since leaving home.

"Smoke?"

Carl was offering him a cigarette. He shook his head, "No, thanks."

"Go ahead. I've got more."

"No, I don't smoke. Thanks anyway."

"You're lucky," Carl remarked. "Smokes are damn scarce in here." He lit the cigarette himself, snapping the match at the can. "Unless you got money. You got any money?"

"Sure," Doug lied. He didn't trust Carl, and he wasn't going to show him any weakness.

"That's good," Carl approved, but he didn't look very happy. He made a sucking sound, cleaning his teeth with his tongue.

An electric babble of Spanish sounded in the tank. Even though he couldn't understand a word of the language, Doug knew something serious was happening. Carl padded out, still barefooted, and Doug followed him.

A man was backing towards them and a young Mexican with a smooth face was stalking him, crouched over, holding a jagged piece of metal, slowly twisting it as he moved forward.

It was a cup, Doug realized with an unpleasant shock, a cup that had been bent and smashed until it had split open forming a primitive knife.

The man on the defensive turned a little and Doug saw that he was an older Mexican with a thin, ragged beard.

"Te rajastes," the young Mexican said, shaking the cup at the older man's face. The young Mexican's face was completely blank and his eyes were half closed.

A tall man in an undershirt stepped out and put his hand on the young Mexican's arm. He started to say something but the boy whirled and slashed at him before he could get his mouth open. He jumped back, staring at the red line across the back of his hand as if he couldn't believe it was there. He didn't move again.

Doug watched the older Mexican, wondering if he would fight, but Doug could smell his fear and that bothered him. He was a man. He should fight, but Doug sensed he wasn't going to.

The man inched back, watching the cup. He bumped against one of the tables. Apparently it unnerved him when he found his retreat cut off, because he turned away and backed up against the bars. Realizing he was trapped, he held his hands out, fingers spread.

"No lo hice aldrede, Armando, me maderiaron." His face was yellowish and his eyes moved up and down with the cup.

"¡Hijo de puta!" the young Mexican swore softly. *"Aldrede o no...."* He stepped in and brought the cup up in a swift arc.

"Por Diosito," the older Mexican begged, and turning, he tried to climb the bars.

The cup caught him on the edge of the jaw and tore up into his cheek. He began to fall off the bars and the backhand slash that followed tore across his forehead, grating against the bone.

"¡Madre!" He screamed and dropped to the floor, with his arms covering his head.

The young Mexican jumped in and kicked him twice, deliberately aiming for the groin. Then he stood back and said, *"Por mi hermano,"* and walked quickly away. The crowd moved aside for him.

The tank was full of men who had rushed out to watch, shocked into silence by the swiftness and violence of the attack. Now they turned away in a rising sound of comment. No one went near the man on the floor.

Doug relaxed his hands. He'd had them clenched so tightly they ached. His palms were sweaty and he wiped them on his pants. The man on the floor began to make a bubbling noise.

"Shouldn't we help him?" Doug asked Carl.

"Do your own time," Carl told him shortly.

Carl went back to his bunk and started putting on his socks, but Doug paused in the cell door looking back. He still felt he should try to do something, but he couldn't walk through the circle of silence around the wounded Mexican.

As Doug watched, the man lifted his head and stared at the blood on his hands. It seemed to horrify him. He made a hollow gulping sound. He got up and shuffled to the door at the end of the tank and rattled it, calling in English, "Doctor! Doctor!"

The tank was suddenly empty and the men were quiet in their cells. Doug climbed into his bunk and turned to the wall. Wrapping his arms around his head, he tried to control his trembling.

He heard Billy above him. "What's all the racket?"

"Someone got cut," Carl said. He was stomping his heel down into a cowboy boot.

"Who?"

"Some wetback. Your little buddy Armando cut him."

"You mean Agnes's buddy." Billy's voice grew cautious, and he added quietly, "He ain't no buddy of mine."

The yelling and the rattling went on, and Billy jumped down

from his bunk and sat on the can. "I wish they'd get him out of here so he'd stop that goddam banging. That Agnes could sleep through anything. Look at him."

"I've seen him," Carl replied dryly. He pulled a battered magazine from under his mattress and settled down with it, ignoring Billy. There was a slamming noise, followed by shuffling. Then it was quiet.

Billy said, "I bet those bulls tear this tank apart."

Carl grunted and said, "Not for a wetback."

After awhile Billy asked, "What they got you for?"

It was a moment before Doug realized Billy was talking to him. He rolled over, surprised.

"They caught me in a store."

"Yeah? What were you doing in there?"

Carl broke in, "Buying a posey."

"Shit," Billy said. "You act like we was all here for a bank robbery."

"I don't care if you're here for carrying a concealed sandwich. What's the sense of talking about it?"

Billy put on his pants and wandered out into the tank. Doug tapped his foot against the wall and wished that he'd never come anywhere near Ardilla. Time passed, and he thought about the same things over and over again. He began to wonder what was going to happen to him, but he didn't want to think about that. He pulled his watch out of his pocket, holding it cupped in his hand. It surprised him that it was after ten already. Turned to the wall he began to wind the watch. Something made him look up, and he saw Billy watching him through the bars. When their eyes met Billy turned and entered the cell. Doug heard him climbing into his own bunk.

Carl sat up and took a flat box from under his mattress. Doug saw that there was candy in it, and realized how hungry he was. Carl threw him a bar.

"Don't tell me you don't eat candy."

It was an Oh Henry bar. Doug could feel it through the stiff wrapper.

"Go on, eat it," Carl urged him. He said it almost harshly, but he had a funny, tentative look on his face. There was something young and uncertain within the creased red skin, and Doug saw that Carl probably wasn't as old as he seemed, maybe only in his forties.

Billy's head appeared over the edge of the bunk. He looked at the candy and grinned. "Better be careful of this old man. I never thought I'd see him throwing candy bars around."

"I ain't throwing it around," Carl said suddenly. He turned away and picked up his magazine. Doug knew the joke Billy was trying to make, and he didn't like it, but he didn't say anything. He ate the candy and threw the wrapper in the toilet.

Sitting on the end of his bunk, he looked out one of the windows. He could see the roof of a building and part of a sign. The sky was as empty as a blue wall.

He kept thinking about Agnes, wondering when he was going to wake up. He was afraid that whatever happened he wouldn't handle himself well. He didn't think he wanted to be tough, or important, or anything like that. He just wanted people to know he was all right.

"*Severson.*" A loudspeaker was blasting.

He heard it twice before he realized it was his name. Turning to Carl, he asked, "What's that?"

"Probably questioning," Carl told him.

Carl didn't look up from his magazine, so Doug quickly hid his watch under his mattress.

CHAPTER SIX

They took him into a small room. It was empty except for a table and three chairs. The table had a scarred linoleum top and the walls were the color of custard.

Through a barred window Doug saw the top of a palm tree. The smaller plainclothesman threw a folder on the table.

He gave Doug a brief sizing-up, as if he were measuring a job. Then he smiled and indicated one of the chairs. "This is Bailey Johnson, and I'm Bob Terrel. There's a few things we want to find out."

They both wore hats. Terrel was a bland, quiet-speaking man, dressed like a cop would dress in Portland or Sacramento. Bailey Johnson was something else. He wore green whipcord pants held by a three-inch black belt. The belt was fastened with a large silver buckle, elaborately mounted with turquoise and abalone. His tie clasp was a replica of a handgun, and his hatband was woven of rawhide. His face was bent on the awkward bones of his skull, and in the taut hollows below the ridge of his cheeks, the flesh was pitted with old acne scars. His eyes were indifferent.

He leaned against the wall and crossed his arms over his chest. His hands were large, the knuckles swollen. He seemed to be thinking of something else.

After one look at Bailey Johnson, Doug kept his eyes on Terrel.

Terrel sat down across from him and pushed his hat back with the heel of his palm. His hair was curly and it dropped over his forehead. With his brown eyes it made him look like he might be part Italian or maybe Spanish. "It doesn't look like you're from around here," he said.

It was a statement, but Doug answered, "Yes, sir." His voice sounded low and meek. He heard Johnson moving around behind him. Then he heard him speak.

"Just dropped in to do a little stealing?"

Johnson sounded mad. Doug didn't answer. There wasn't any right answer.

Terrel took a square tan card out of the folder. He read, tapping the card gently with his index finger. He nodded as if he agreed with what was on the card.

Doug was uncomfortably aware of the other cop behind him. His nose must have been obstructed in some way because Doug could hear him breathing.

Terrel looked up. "You say you're from Sacramento, California? What're you doing down here?"

"Just looking around."

"Looking for work?"

Doug heard a snort behind him. He flinched.

"How long you been in town?" Terrel asked.

"I just got here last night—"

"Bullshit!"

That was Johnson. Doug felt his face growing hot.

Terrel snapped the card in his hands and tossed it on the table. "We had a report on you a week ago. Prowling. A young kid. Red plaid jacket, white shoes. It seems to fit."

"It fits all right," Johnson said from behind him.

Doug was bewildered. He was ready to admit breaking into the feed store. What difference did it make whether he admitted it? They'd caught him at it. He couldn't understand what they were getting at.

"Look," he began anxiously, "I came on the bus from Phoenix. Last night. I—"

A stunning pain caught him behind his ears. Not a blow, just a steady pressure. His mouth was open and he was aware that he was trying to make some kind of a noise, but he couldn't hear anything.

Then it stopped suddenly, and he was all right.

Terrel looked grave. "Don't do that, Bailey," he said mildly. "He doesn't mean to lie."

"There was a cop!" The words jumped out of his mouth. "Right by the depot. He saw me get off the bus. Honest. You can ask him."

"We happen to know better," Bailey said.

"But he saw me," Doug insisted, turning to look up at the cop behind him. He saw the big hand, and then his head was wrenched to the front. The pain seemed to last longer. When it was over he was bitterly surprised to find his eyes wet.

"That's enough of that," Terrel said sharply. "Can't you see he's just a kid? Let me try and talk to him."

Johnson made a disgusted noise, but he moved around and took the third chair. He stretched out, crossing his ankles, and started rolling a Bull Durham cigarette. "I don't know why you want to baby these little snakes."

"Cigarette?"

Terrel was offering him a red pack. "No... thanks."

"How old are you really?"

That was his out. But he couldn't take it. "Eighteen," he said as firmly as he could.

Terrel lit up. He started to talk quietly, gesturing with his cigarette.

"We know you've been in town for at least a week, so let's just pass that for awhile. OK? Now, here's what you look like to us. We know you didn't start pulling burglaries last night. You knew what you were doing. You almost had the cash drawer pried open—pretty good job too."

Terrel smiled at that, showing he wasn't stuffy, that it was all open between them like friends talking about something that wasn't very important, but Doug was too confused to respond. He heard a clicking noise and jerked to the side.

Johnson was using a Zippo lighter on his brown-paper cigarette. In his hand the lighter seemed half size. He snapped it shut and looked up, blowing smoke through his nose.

Terrel went on explaining earnestly, and Doug began to understand. They wanted him to admit some other jobs, things that had happened before he came to town. Terrel described the jobs briefly, told him they knew they were his work, but that it didn't matter to them as long as he helped clean them up, and what difference did it make to him since he was already caught?

That was right. What difference did it make? They could only send him to prison once. It all seemed very logical, but he didn't like it. He stole, sure, but he wasn't that kind of a thief, breaking into places night after night. That there was difference seemed obvious to him.

Terrel paused and leaned across the table. "You understand?

It isn't going to make any difference in the way the judge handles you, because we won't even file these as charges. All we want to do is clear our books. OK?"

Doug couldn't say yes or no. He avoided Terrel's eyes.

"You want to tell us about them?" Terrel persisted.

Johnson walked behind him, and Doug felt his shoulders lifting to protect his neck, but Johnson only went to the window, opened it, and snapped his cigarette butt out. The distant sound of cars came into the room, and down in the street someone was laughing. The laugh seemed incredible.

Terrel opened the folder and pulled out a sheaf of closely typed forms. "Maybe this will help you remember. What about a garage over on One-sixty Ajo Street? You made entry through a back window the same as you did last night."

"I don't even know where that is."

"I'm damned if I know why you're fooling around with this punk," Johnson said.

But Terrel went on patiently: "You could have been over there without knowing where you were, couldn't you? The safe was tampered with, but it was too much for you so you broke open the cigarette machine. Remember?"

Doug tried not to answer, but then he heard Johnson close the window, and the silence began pushing him. He started to rub his hands together, harder and harder. He had to say something and he was afraid to say no.

"Maybe—"

Terrel smiled. "That's better."

After that it was like he was helping Terrel prove something to Johnson, like they were both against the big bastard. In rapid succession he copped out to three more jobs.

The last job he admitted was a house burglary. A ring had been stolen. Some other things too, but the ring was important to the houseowner. It was a gift to his wife and he'd made a big point of it during the initial investigation because his wife had died recently. Terrel wanted to know where the ring was because he knew Doug wouldn't want to keep something so important to this other man.

Doug saw the trap he was in. He tried to say he hadn't seen it, but Terrel wouldn't take that answer. He described the ring in detail, looking earnestly at Doug as if he only needed to be reminded what the ring looked like in order to remember where it was. Terrel's expression said, Don't let me down now, I'm trying to help you.

"I didn't see it," Doug repeated miserably. He found himself squeezing his hands together.

"That doesn't make sense. It was with some other stuff that's missing. A watch and some cuff links. Did you sell them?"

"No."

"Did you hide them somewhere?"

"I didn't take it." His voice dropped to a whisper.

"What?"

"I said I didn't take it."

Terrel slapped the table with his palm, and blew his breath out in exasperation. "Look, Doug, all the guy wants is to get the ring back. He doesn't care who took it or what happens to them, but the ring is important to him. If you sold it, we'll get it back."

"I didn't sell it."

"Did you throw it somewhere?"

Suddenly Doug was yelling, *"No! No!* I didn't *take* it! I told you I didn't *take* it—"

"Dammit, that doesn't make sense. If you were in there, you must have—"

"I didn't take it. I didn't take anything. I didn't do any of those things."

Doug stopped, staring angrily at Terrel, and he saw a funny bored look come into the cop's eyes. There was a moment of ugly silence. Then Johnson said, "I'll handle this."

He spun Doug around and slapped him.

Then he balled his fists and said, "Believe me, kid, that's nothing. I don't want to hear any more of your crap. You're not in the Boy Scouts now. If you're old enough to sneak around in the night and bust into places, you're goddam well old enough to take your lumps. You admitted them jobs. And you did them. Right?"

Doug glanced at Terrel, but Terrel wasn't even looking at him. He was twisting a paper clip and frowning like he was watching a bad movie. Johnson said softly, "You wouldn't cop to something you didn't do, would you?"

Doug shook his head. He couldn't make his mouth move.

"Then you did pull those jobs?"

Numbly Doug nodded, hoping just to buy a few minutes' peace.

"Speak up, kid, I want to hear you say something."

"Yes."

"Yes what?"

"I broke into those places."

"All right."

That was the end of it. Terrel told him they'd fix up a statement for him to sign, and that they were going to check up on his past. The address he had given in Sacramento was a phony, but he didn't have to worry about that, because Johnson tapped him on the chest and told him that they'd give him a day or two to remember where the ring was, but that was all.

"I want that ring," Johnson said. "And next time we come up here to talk you're going to tell me what you did with it."

CHAPTER SEVEN

Agnes woke up while Doug was out. Noticing the empty blankets in the fourth bunk, he asked, "Where's that kid?"

Billy answered, "Out to questioning, I think."

"Questioning? Jesus, Billy, did you just let him waltz out?"

Billy shot a warning look down at Carl. "I talked to him. He's all right."

"All right? How do you know he's all right? If they push

him he's liable to crack in a thousand places."

Billy leaned across the space between their bunks and whispered, "What would you have done? Was I supposed to kill him or something?"

Agnes scowled, but he didn't answer.

Billy went on, "He's all right. Just a young kid. He's still got dew on him. Carl even got up off a candy bar."

"Yeah?" Agnes grinned. "Carl, you old mother fucker, you're just plain evil."

"I ain't going to be too many of them mother fuckers," Carl replied in a peevish monotone.

Agness flopped over and looked down at Carl, intending to ride him, but Billy broke in with the news. "Armando cut someone a little while ago."

"What?" Agnes asked quietly.

"Another Chicano. They pulled him out of the tank."

"Armando."

"No, the other guy. I was asleep so I didn't see it."

"He cut his face up," Carl added briefly.

Agnes frowned and sat up in bed, smoothing his hair with both hands, running his fingers around to the back of his head.

"He ought to have more sense than that," he said quietly to Billy. "Did the bulls make a fuss?"

"No, they just took him out."

"Armando takes some chances."

Agnes pulled his Levis off the chain above his head and slipped his legs into them. He jumped to the floor to finish pulling them up, closing the top snap three inches below his flat navel. He grabbed a ragged towel and told Billy, "I'm going to shower."

Billy followed him out of the cell, and they stopped in front of one of the tables. Agnes picked up a worn deck of cards and cut them a couple of times with a practiced flourish.

"What do you think about that kid?"

Billy shrugged. "It'd be better if he didn't know, but I don't think we have to worry. We may not have anything to worry about. I saw Slim this morning."

Agnes slapped the cards sharply in his palm.

"Yeah?"

"He says he's got to have more cigarettes. He says it's pretty touchy, and—"

"That miserable bastard!"

Agnes found himself glaring at Billy as if it was his fault, and he turned away scattering the cards on the table.

"Well, that just about does it. How much did he up it?"

"To six cartons."

"Why not sixty? What does he think we want? Gold hacksaws?"

"He says they're hard to get at, and—"

"Oh, screw what he says. How do we know? He's got us by the balls."

"What are we going to do?" Billy asked with open anxiety.

"I don't know."

Billy rubbed the bumps along his jawline, waiting for Agnes to think of something. But Agnes just stared at the bars as if he'd like to tear them out. Finally he slammed his fist into his palm. "I'm going to take a bath."

The cells were in two banks of six each. Between them was a small space about four by five feet. Here the mops were racked beside an old laundry sink stained with orange-and-gray discolorations. The floor was always cold and slippery with soap, and usually someone's socks were soaking in the sink. The shower was in the back, a metal box of half-inch boiler plate.

Agnes stood in the shower, stunned by the thick steam of hot water. He found a sliver of yellow laundry soap under worn floorboards, and as he rubbed a thin lather over the solid muscles of his chest and arms, he began to whistle.

His name wasn't Agnes. Agnes was a jail nickname he'd picked up. Not because of any suggestion of effeminacy, but probably because of his complete maleness and the grinning sense of fun with which he had first accepted the joke name.

He was twenty-two, but he looked a few years older because he'd been raised in the open, squinting against the sun in the summer fields. It was part of his bringing up that he could run and shoot and Indian wrestle. He was short, but not so short as to be very sensitive about it, and his face was lean and handsome. His hair was very full, long and still sun-streaked, and his skin was still tan. His wide chest rose in a definite V from his narrow waist, and over his right nipple he had tat-tooed "Beer" and over his left, "Wine." On his shoulder were the initials R.I.S. which stood for Ranson Industrial School. It was at this school that the tattooing had been done. He'd gone in for it because everyone else had, working on each other with a needle wrapped in thread and dipped in a bottle of stolen India ink. At the time the tattoos had been a most solemn badge, but afterwards he seldom remembered he had them. Sometimes, as now when he was showering, he would really see them and think they were kind of silly. Sometimes girls mentioned them and, grinning, he would offer them the "Beer" nipple, saying the "Wine" was for high-class broads.

Agnes was Billy's crime partner, and his buddy for over five years. Each had something to give the other. Billy was almost ugly—with his big ears and his bad skin—so Agnes was the honey that caught the girls. And they usually seemed to be in similar pairs. One pretty and one not so pretty. Billy always ended up with the plain one.

For his share Billy always saved some money. So when Agnes would say, "If we only had a few bucks—" Billy would grin and reach for his pocket. Also Billy was handy. He could make anything run that had wheels, and when it was running he'd drive it for hour after hour while Agnes slept or hooted out the window. All Billy needed in the way of reward was for Agnes to say, "Buddy, you wheel this thing like you grew up in it."

It never occurred to either one of them that this was an in-adequate basis for friendship.

Now they had taken their first bad fall, hundreds of miles from home. A month before they had held up a market without bothering to discover that Ardilla was one-gutted. It was a small job, just for gas and eating money, but their car had been identified, and when they tried to drive out of town a few hours later they were trapped on the single road.

Now they were waiting trial, but they didn't plan on hanging around for it. From the moment they hit the jail, Agnes had started looking for a way out. Billy helped him. After a week of poking around they decided that all they needed was a couple of hacksaws. Agnes propositioned Slim, but Slim wanted three cartons. He said he didn't mind helping, but he wasn't going to stick his neck out for nothing. Agnes and Billy had wasted what little money they did have and so they could only raise a carton. So Agnes brought Armando in with the other two.

Now Slim was demanding six, and Agnes didn't have any idea where he was going to get them. He knew it would be up to him. Billy was helpless when it came to anything like this.

Agnes dried himself. Standing with his feet apart, he sawed at his body with the towel, ticking off names and faces in his head. Someone was going to lose. He didn't know who yet.

When he finished, he hurried to another cell and looked in. The bulb was unscrewed and the cell was shadowed.

"Que pasa, Armando?"

The young Mexican was curled in the top bunk. His eyes moved slowly to Agnes. *"Nada."* His voice was husky.

Agnes stepped inside. Armando's cell was empty except for Armando himself. "What'd you get into this morning, *ese?*"

"A snitch, man. From before. Goddam *amarillo*, he ratted on my brother in El Paso. I waited on him until I was sure, then I cut him."

Agnes shook his head. "You might have killed him. Then where would he be?"

"If I'd meant to kill him, he'd be dead right now. I just wanted to cut him. That's all."

Agnes couldn't see Armando's face clearly, but he knew the Mexican meant what he was saying. Armando was quiet and remote like a lizard in a shadow, and like that lizard he was capable of a vivid swiftness. Agnes liked Armando because he had won his trust and a few of his almost sweetly girlish Mexican smiles. He liked him because Agnes liked most people except squares, finks, and queers.

"You got any more stuff?" Agnes asked.

Armando sat up quickly, his eyes bright and worried in his opaque face. "What's the matter?"

Agnes told him the price had gone up, and Armando's face didn't seem to change, but suddenly it was different—cold as a wet stone. "You got everything I had."

"Can you borrow from someone? Someone you don't mind burning?"

Armando shook his head slowly, his eyes half closed. "No one." He was silent for a moment, then he murmured, "*Gavacho cabrone....* You know, man, they probably going to send me up next week."

"Can't you get it put off?"

"Hell no, man, my lawyer ask for too damn many postponements now. I tell you, they going to send me sure."

Agnes smiled and gave him the "sure-in" sign with his fist. "Don't worry, buddy, we'll make it one way or another. I'll take care of it."

Armando stretched out and frowned at the ceiling. "You trust that guy?"

"Slim?"

"Yeah."

"Can't do nothing but trust him. He's supposed to be an old con. He talks like he's been around enough. He's probably all right."

"He better be. I tell you one thing, man, I be getting out some day, and if he screws us up—" Armando made a swift knifelike motion and his lips parted over his teeth. "I ain't kidding, man, I kill him quick."

Agnes shrugged it off. He didn't want to think about anything going wrong. Maybe Slim had a right to more money. Agnes didn't like it. He had no talent for the trade of money and he hated to bargain, but he didn't mistrust a man just because he was on the make. He reached over and squeezed Armando's arm. "Don't sweat it. What'd you use on that guy this morning?"

"My cup. I stomped it till it split open."

Agnes grinned. "Now what're you going to drink out of?"

"I don't know, man. My hands, I guess."

"Not coffee, I'll get you a cup. They put some kid in our cell last night—I'll cop his."

"Thanks."

"That's nothing—I'd better get hustling and see what 1 can turn up."

A poker game was going at one of the tables, the same game that went on every day; Agnes paused behind the players, watching the faded red cards flick on the gray table. The stakes were tobacco, but there wasn't a carton in play; as the game went on the same cigarettes were won and lost until they became too battered to smoke.

There was one man at the table who might have the three cartons. Pesco. He was a big neat man with a lot of dark wavy hair. He habitually wore tinted glasses with heavy black frames, and today he had on a soft white shirt, soiled but obviously expensive. His nails were clean and the gestures with which he handled the cards were precise and elegant.

Agnes took a broken comb out of his back pocket and ran it through his hair. He studied Pesco. He didn't know too much about him except he claimed to be from California and talked like a big wheel. Agnes felt he was probably a phony, but he was friendly with him. To talk to, at least.

Pesco looked up and saw Agnes. He looked around at the other players and said with elaborate casualness, "I didn't think it was noon yet."

Someone answered, "Hell, it ain't eleven o'clock."

"Yeah? Then how come Agnes is up?"

Agnes smiled at the ribbing. "You know what, Pesco—I got the damnedest notion there was some money to be picked up out here."

"Come on in," Pesco offered. "The water's fine."

"The only thing is, I'm broke."

"That's sad, Agnes. That really tears me up."

"I thought maybe you might stake me."

Pesco frowned. "No, I don't think I could do that."

Agnes had expected the answer; still it burnt him. "You come on like Nick the Greek over a pack of cigarettes."

Pesco picked his hand up, peeked at it, then sailed the cards into the center of the table. He smiled, a crisp Italian smile. "Agnes, you're all heart and no logic. If I stake you what can I win from you? My own cigarettes, that's all. But if you should get lucky, I could lose. Does that make sense?"

"If you say so. I still think you're too chicken to play against me."

"Get something to play with. We'll play any game that you can name, for any amount that you can count."

"I will," Agnes said, and somebody else complained, "Deal the cards."

Agnes was angry when he left the game, but by the time he reached the cell, he was all right again.

Billy was dressed and sitting up on his bunk, his expression anxious. His skin seemed dry and pale and the circles under his eyes were a faint yellow. Next to Agnes he looked unhealthy.

"Come on, Billy," Agnes said with a forced casualness, "Let's take a walk around the park."

"Don't wander off," Carl said dryly.

"Did you think of anything?" Billy asked as soon as they were alone.

"Yeah, there's an easy out. I'll take a carton of what we got stashed, and win what we need."

"In the game?"

"Sure."

"What if you lose?" Billy asked bleakly.

"I won't. That game's a pipe."

"That's what you said before, and you lost your shirt. The only one who's got any real money is Pesco. That means you got to beat him and he's a pro."

"Pesco ain't nothing! All he's got is a fancy shuffle and a lot of luck."

"Luck? What does he need with luck? He's got all the dough. He can buy any pot he wants and sandbag as much as he wants to. One bad hand and you're dead. Then what?"

Agnes punched his fist into his palm. "Dammit, we've got to try something. I'm not going to let this slide and go on to the joint like some damn sheep."

"Wait a minute," Billy said quietly. "That kid they put in our cell. He's got a watch."

"Oh, yeah?" Agnes asked with interest. "What kind?"

"I don't know. I didn't see it good. He keeps it in his pocket, but I caught him looking at it. It looks good. Gold."

Agnes looked away, thinking. "He's wise, huh?"

"He doesn't look it. He looks cherry."

"Maybe not so cherry. He probably stole the watch and at least he's got sense enough not to flash it. Let's shake his sack down. He might have stashed it."

Billy hesitated. "We could ride this kid too hard. He's young, but he's pretty good size. I think we could push him too much."

"Listen," Agnes said tensely. "All that matters to us is getting out of here. The rest of it don't mean nothing. I don't care if this kid's a giant, he's got to come off that watch. And if he opens his mouth, I'll waste him. Now, let's take a look."

When they re-entered the cell, Agnes shook Doug's blankets and flipped the mattress up.

Carl asked him, "What are you looking for?"

"Something to read," Agnes told him, covering the watch with his hand. "There were some old magazines under here."

"That someone's bunk now," Carl said pointedly.

Agnes let the mattress fall back, sticking the watch in his pocket as he turned. "Yeah, I know, Carl, and you look out for him. He'll be real grateful."

"What do you mean by that?"

"Just what I said."

The watch was a good one. Agnes knew that even though it wasn't to his taste. It was thin and dudeish looking with little gold dots in place of numbers. But it was easily worth three cartons. Probably more.

Slim was due back with the noon meal and Agnes figured he was ready to deal with him. He didn't know how he was going to deal with him—he didn't think clearly about it, except to caution himself not to get hot. Like it or not he had to play it carefully with Slim.

Still he felt pretty good now. He put on his shirt and paced the concrete between the poker game and the television. Fifteen steps up and fifteen steps back. He could look at the gray bars and the bland cream wall without gritting his teeth, he could stop and watch the women on television without getting a tight sour feeling in his stomach, because he could say to himself, wait till next week.

He was watching the poker game when Doug came back. Agnes looked up at the sound of the tank door and saw the slender kid enter, poking along like he had a lot on his mind. He went into the cell.

Agnes frowned. Carl was in there. After a moment he walked down and leaned against the edge of the cell door, watching and listening. Carl was pumping the kid, trying to find out what had happened, but the kid wasn't saying much.

Ordinarily the kid wouldn't have pushed Agnes one way or another. He wasn't the kind of person Agnes would have paid any attention to. Quiet sounding with a neat smooth face, still unformed by any kind of real living, his bearing was too sub-dued to impress Agnes. He knew that the kid was aware of him as he caught the nervous flicker of his brown eyes, and he smiled tightly, waiting for Carl to shut up. But Carl looked up at him irritably. "Why don't you come in or go out?"

Agnes straightened up, hooking his thumbs in his back pockets. "Am I bothering you?"

"I just wonder what you're standing there for."

"Because I feel like it. Is that a good enough reason?"

Carl didn't answer. He stared at Agnes for a moment, then looked away, slapping his bunk. He stood up.

Agnes set himself, but Carl brushed past him, tucking in his shirt tail. He turned and spoke to the kid. "Come on, let's see what they got on TV."

Doug looked at Agnes and shook his head slowly. "I don't feel much like it."

"Suit yourself. It's kinda crowded in there."

Agnes watched Carl walk away, rolling a little because of his high-heeled boots, then he stepped into the cell. He stood over the kid, and Billy sat up in his bunk.

"You remember what I told you last night?"

Doug was sitting hunched over with his head pulled down into the collar of his jacket. He looked up, pushing his hair out of his eyes.

"I heard you. If that's what you mean."

"You know what I mean."

Agnes liked the way Doug had answered. He had a little pride, and a man with pride doesn't snitch. Agnes sat down on Carl's bunk and leaned back. "Where you been?" he asked in a normal tone.

"Out getting questioned."

"Who questioned you?" Billy asked from above.

"Some guy named Johnson and another guy."

Agnes whistled softly. "Buddy, you drew a beaut. I just know you told him anything he wanted to know. I just hope, for your sake, you left us out of it."

For a moment Doug's glance wavered. Then he settled his jaw and looked Agnes in the eye. "I didn't tell them nothing."

Agnes made a face of humorous doubt. "No?"

"I don't care what you think. I didn't talk to them about anything. And that ain't all."

Doug paused, seeming to make some inner struggle, then he said quickly, "I want my watch back."

Agnes sat up. "What're you talking about?"

"My watch. I'm talking about my watch." Doug pulled his mattress up. "It was right there. One of you guys must have got it."

"Kid, there's over thirty men in this tank. What makes you think—"

"Because he saw it." Doug jerked his head at Billy. "And he's the only one who did see it. The only one who even knew I had it—and don't call me kid. I don't like it."

Agnes stood up, clamping his fists. The muscles corded in his forearms and ridged along his jawline. "You want to get it on? Is that it? You want to have it out right now?" Already Agnes could feel the blood beginning to pound in his ears. At the slightest hint from Doug that he was going to fight, Agnes would have let go, but the kid wilted.

"I just want my watch back, that's all." He sounded ashamed.

"*Your* watch," Agnes sneered. "Where'd you get a watch? I'll tell you. You copped it. Now where you got any squawk coming? You can't lose what don't belong to you."

"It don't belong to you neither."

"It belongs to whoever's got it. And unless you can take it back, you better just forget about it."

Doug didn't say anything.

"You understand?"

The kid was looking at the floor, his hands wrapped together.

Agnes rose on the balls of his feet. "Well?"

"I understand."

"All right."

Agnes vaulted into his own bunk. It took him a minute to cool off, then he rolled over and winked at Billy.

"Almost chowtime?"

Fifteen minutes later, Agnes heard the first sounds telling him that chow was coming—the clatter of a dipper against the side of a pot and the rattle of metal wheels shimmying against their axles. The sound was unmistakable, and Agnes shouted, "Here we go," sliding off his bunk and rushing out into the corridor. Through the round port in the tank door, he saw Slim and the little trusty they called Corky. They were standing beside the chow wagon waiting for the deputy to open the gate into the outer corridor. He tried to signal Slim, but his head was turned the other way.

"Is that chow?" Pesco called from the poker game.

Agnes spun around. "Goddam betcha!"

Someone else at the game shouted a wordless approval, and a dry voice said, "Son, you must really be hungry."

Men came out of their cells, looking toward the end of the tank. Then they began to crowd around the feeding slot.

Agnes ducked back into the cell. Carl was there, so he just shrugged at Billy. Billy whispered, "What'd he say?"

"I didn't get a chance to talk to him. For Christ's sake, Billy, they're still outside." He punched Billy's mattress. "He'll do it. He's got to."

Agnes went back out and watched them wheel the cart along the other side of the bars. Zack the regular day jailer was with them. Zack took a position at the head of the cart where he could monitor the amount of food given to each man. That was fine as long as he watched the food. Agnes shoved through and got a bowl of beans. Then he went back to the cell for his cup. Slim was working his way along the tank, pouring coffee as the men held their cups up to the bars. Agnes followed him.

Near the far end of the tank, away from the deputy, the men thinned out, and Agnes put his face up against the bars and whispered, "Slim. Hey, Slim."

Slim looked up, still pouring. His face showed a brief warning. He moved up to Agnes and pretended to pour.

"Well, what're you going to do?"

"You trying to get rich?" Agnes hadn't intended to say that, but that's what came out. He hated sucking up to Slim.

"Listen," Slim demanded. "Do you know what I'm up against? Do you know anything about it? You want me to do something? All right, I'm telling you what it costs."

"What'd you jump the price for?"

Slim took a tone of elaborate patience. "You know, Agnes, I don't manufacture hacksaw blades. I have to get them from someone else. When his price goes up, mine goes up too. This is a little more complicated than running down to the store."

Agnes didn't really believe him, but he felt a little jiggle of doubt. "You can get them?"

"Yes, I can get them. At my price. Can you get it up?"

Agnes smiled. He felt that this was his trick. "Don't worry, I've got it." He pulled the watch out of his pocket, and held it where Slim could see it. "I've got three cartons and this—"

Slim shifted the coffee pot and held his hand out. "Let me see it."

Agnes shook his head. "You're seeing it."

"OK, play it that way. What do you think that's worth to me?"

"It's worth whatever one of those fat-ass cops'll give you for it, and it'll sure in hell be more than three cartons."

Slim looked at the watch closely. "Maybe," he agreed cautiously. "You got the cigarettes ready?"

"I told you I had them, didn't I? Now when can we get some action?"

Slim glanced down to check up on the jailer and found him still watching the feeding.

"Maybe tomorrow."

"Don't fool with me, man. Can I count on that?"

"I said maybe." Slim turned and looked at the jailer again. When he turned back to Agnes his face had changed: it seemed grayer and tighter. His eyes were angry.

"Look, kid, I'll tell you something—I hope you beat them.

I hope you let everyone out. You have that stuff ready tomorrow, I'll see what I can do for you."

Slim started away, his shoulders pulled over by the weight of the pot; his bitter eyes were still on Zack. Agnes took a couple of quick steps and jumped up to the bars alongside of him. "Take it easy," he whispered, and Slim nodded slightly, still moving away.

Now that's action for sure, Agnes thought—one more day won't kill us.

He turned back towards his own cell and for the first time he noticed a man sitting a few feet away, eating his beans. His position was such that he couldn't have helped overhearing. Agnes pounded his fists in disgust. That was what he hated about jail, you couldn't walk without tripping over some fool. They were everywhere you looked.

The man wore rimless glasses and a necktie; his hair was neatly parted and his whole attitude was one of not having heard anything, of not wanting to hear anything. Too much so. He had heard.

Agnes looked at him closely and thought, So what? He was only some harmless boob, probably in for drunk driving or child support. He wouldn't even know what it was he'd heard.

CHAPTER EIGHT

Agnes was right. Frazier didn't understand what he'd heard. He'd been listening simply because he was curious, endlessly and idly curious about all the things that happened around him. But he wasn't involved.

Frazier was like an archaeologist puzzling over a fragment of bone as he played a game with himself, trying to deduce a man's life from his clothes and a passing expression, or trying to reconstruct an incident from a few overheard words—and like the archaeologist's, his interest was abstract. He didn't care.

His name had been Frazier for less than a month. Before that it was Randall, and before that, Thornton. He knew and avoided the tendency to pick an alias that was similar to his true name, or even to retain the same initials, but his own tendency—which he never suspected—was to choose names with a faint gloss of English refinement. He would never have used a name like Cline-Smith or Montmercy, but he had called himself Elsworth Wright and Theodore Chetley, among many others. He was Frazier now, Lawrence Frazier, because that was the name he had signed on his last batch of bogus checks. He wasn't, as Agnes thought, a drunk driver, but a wandering forger, and his honest, faintly genteel look was part of his unconscious stock-in-trade.

It was all new to him—his first time—and he felt the shock of a completely different place. It was as if he had been abandoned among a savage tribe, a tribe with language, culture and rituals completely outside his experience.

After five weeks in jail, Frazier's poise was still intact. He was still in the tank, but not of it. It was still only something to speculate about.

Now he idly pieced over the conversation he had heard. He didn't know Slim except as a face, and he saw Agnes as a young tribesman, self-confident simply because he was so superficial, loud, brisk, and empty. He'd heard enough to know that it rang with some basic tension, and that made it interesting. What could he be that caught up in? But then he realized that it might not take much to excite Agnes—he was usually yelling about something. Frazier smiled at the progression of his own thoughts.

He washed his bowl and spoon and put them up by the tank door. There was a slot in the door through which he dropped the spoon. He returned to the same seat and lit a cigarette, smoked it for awhile and then put it out. Carefully flicking the dead ash away, he replaced it in the pack. Four more days until the commissary wagon came and he had thirty-six and a half cigarettes: four into thirty-six—skip the half—that was nine a day. But really it was a little over four days, since commissary didn't come until late afternoon, so it was actually four-point-five, and that came out to eight even. Three after each meal, that left... Escape! The idea suddenly slid out of his subconscious. And as soon as it was formed he accepted it as obvious—what was the most valuable thing in jail for a youngster like Agnes? To get out. But how could he manage that?

Frazier looked around the tank, and everywhere he looked he saw metal and concrete. It wasn't possible. The whole idea frightened him. He remembered seeing Agnes on a half a dozen different occasions talking with the Spanish kid who had caused the trouble just this morning, and that started him thinking about violence.

Frazier stood up uneasily and peered around the tangle at the poker game, but he couldn't see Agnes. A thin haze of smoke drifted up from the game, and the players were tense and explosive, slamming the cards and arguing in loud voices. Frazier sensed violence. They must be planning violence. The police might end up shooting into the tank, the shattered bullets whining back and forth against the metal walls. He thought of a ragged lump of lead hitting him—

Frazier deliberately pushed away the beginning of panic and in a moment he was almost as calm as usual, but he didn't watch the afternoon shows on television as he was accustomed to do. He went into his cell and settled on his bunk, his hands neatly clasped on his chest.

Somebody banged a wall down the tank and it boomed hollowly. Frazier sat up quickly, one hand kneading the fist of the other. He listened intently. Nothing followed. He got up and looked out into the tank. Everything was just as it had been. He settled down again, but detachment was impossible now. He heard the tank around him, minute by minute.

The man on the bunk across from Frazier was breathing heavily as if his nose were half-clogged, but his face was passive. He was reading a coverless book, bent double in one large hand, a heavy-faced old man with a swollen body. His name was Tharp and he was sixty-seven years old.

"Tharp—" Frazier said hesitantly, then suddenly was resolved. "Tharp, do you know that boy they call Agnes?"

"Huh?"

Frazier repeated his question and Tharp's slow eyes turned to him, dull as the eyes of an old sheep. "The one they call Agnes?" Tharp asked.

"Yes. Agnes." Frazier was regretting that he'd started the conversation.

"Sure, I seen him around. What about him?"

"Oh, nothing, really. I was just wondering about him."

"Don't know nothing special about him. He's just one more wild kid." Tharp stopped talking, but he continued to look at Frazier.

Frazier had an impulse to grab his head and stick it back in his book. Instead he said, "I think he's trying to escape."

"Agnes?"

"Yes, Agnes! I overheard him talking to one of the trustys, that thin one with the gray hair, and I'm sure that's what they were talking about. Planning some sort of an escape."

Tharp appeared to think for a moment. Then he said, "I wouldn't pay no attention to it. Someone's always planning something like that. All the places I ever did time there was usually someone talking about it, but you know what?" Tharp smiled slowly. "Ain't any of them ever did anything. I think it helps them to talk about it. Makes the time pass. They keep putting it off and pretty soon they got their time half in; then they can forget about it. Once in awhile someone really tries it. But not often."

CHAPTER NINE

"No shit, you really dummied up on Johnson?"

Agnes was squatting on his heels beside Doug's bunk. The afternoon was as hot as the night before had been cold. The sun poured through the narrow windows and broke against the bars and the tank stifled in the harsh light. Agnes had his shirt off and his flesh seemed damp. He was smiling easily, just as if nothing had happened between them.

Doug sat up. He remembered his watch, but it didn't seem as important as it had. "Sure I did."

Agnes grinned. "I sure would like to have seen that. I bet he swelled up like a toad."

Billy climbed down and sat on the can. "Those are the same two that questioned us. Terrel and Johnson."

"They're real cute," Agnes added. Doug watched him shift around and sit on the floor with his back up against Carl's bunk, and he realized Agnes wanted to talk.

"Yeah, they're a pair of dandies," Agnes went on. "They thought they had a couple of old country boys. You know what they tried to pull on us? The big one, he plays the heavy, and the other guy says, 'Oh, come on, Bailey, these kids are all right. Don't rough 'em up.' And the big bastard roars like a lion and acts like he's about ready to tear your head off and stuff it up your ass but the nice guy stops him, and about this time you're so grateful to the nice guy you tell him anything he wants to hear—he's such a nice guy, and you know what? It's all a routine."

"They work it pretty good," Billy said.

"Yeah, those guys should have been actors instead of cops. That's the oldest routine in the hills and that big cop almost had me going for it. I thought he was going to kill me. But pretty soon he gave up and said, 'You're a wise punk, aren't you?' and I told him, 'Well, it's been awhile since I was on a snipe hunt,' and I'm damned if that big bastard didn't laugh."

Doug felt like a fool.

Agnes looked at him and said, "I bet they thought you were a natural. They probably thought you were going to cop out to every job pulled in this country in the last fifteen years. Did they blow it when you gave them a hard time?"

"Boy, did they." Doug knew what Agnes wanted to hear.

Agnes grinned at Billy. "Isn't that a crack-up? I bet he gave those two clowns a fit."

Doug was grinning and nodding himself.

Carl threw his magazine on the floor and lifted up on one elbow. "Well, they haven't got in their last lick. That's one thing you can count on. They can afford to wait. They're not spending their nights in a cell." Carl stared bleakly at Doug, and Doug felt the same revulsion he had sensed that morning. Carl's face was even redder in the heat, except for his temples, they were pale, and the skin looked soft and wet. Doug felt his smile shrivel, but Carl went right on. "By the time you've been here a couple of weeks, you'll be so anxious to talk to someone, you'll tell them anything they want to hear. You'll make up things to tell them."

Agnes didn't look at Carl. "Don't let this sour old bastard get to you," he told Doug. "Billy and I been here over three weeks and all we've ever told any of them is go screw your-selves. Ain't that right, Billy?"

"That's right. Agnes is telling you right." Billy started laugh-ing. "Agnes even told the judge. The judge asked him how did he plead, and Agnes said he wasn't pleading at all, said he hadn't ever done any pleading in his life and he didn't intend to start now. And that judge got red and started beating with that hammer of his. I don't think he likes Agnes any more."

Agnes grinned proudly. "That judge's estimation don't move me much. Besides, I don't think he cared about us going in."

Carl said heavily, "That judge is the meanest man in this country, and when he gets done slugging it to you, you'll have had it. Agnes, you're an old man and you don't even know it."

Agnes turned around and looked at Carl. Doug felt the heat

between them and he hoped Agnes would really tell Carl, but Agnes just said, "Maybe."

"Maybe?" Carl smiled in sour disgust. "For Christ's sake, they got you dead bang with the money in your pocket, a red-hot pistol in your hand, and a line of witnesses a mile long who just can't wait to say, 'He's the man.' Now where's there any maybe in that?"

"All I said was maybe and that's what I meant—maybe. You don't know everything, old man, just 'cause you done thirty years."

Carl made a disgusted sound. "I'd hate to do your Sundays."

"I don't see where you're in such hot shape yourself, old man." Anger was beginning to gather in Agnes's voice, and Doug looked back at Carl to see how he'd take it, but Carl's eyes were quiet and funny again. Both Carl and Agnes had blue eyes. Agnes's eyes were blue like automobile enamel baked in the sun, hard and shiny, all surface, but Carl's eyes seemed to go into some deeper level, and Doug could see something vulnerable in them like the reflection of distant pain. This confused him because he didn't want to feel sympathy for Carl. He knew his feeling was all upside down. Carl had tried to be friendly to him in his way, and even now in Agnes's pocket he could see an outline that was probably his watch—and he still wanted to see Agnes hurt Carl.

Carl answered quietly, "I don't know what my shape has got to do with it. Maybe I'm not in such good shape, but at least I'm not advising some kid to tell the police where to go. All that could possibly buy him is a broken head."

"What's he s'pose to do? Get all cozy with them? Maybe give Johnson a great big slobbery kiss and whisper all his secrets in their ears—"

"Did I say that? What's that got to do with calling them a bagful of sonsabitches?"

Agnes stood up quickly. "OK. That's enough. That's what I think they are and that's what I'm going to say—"

"Until they stomp your teeth out. Then you'll have some trouble."

Agnes didn't answer. Doug saw him opening and closing his hands. A muscle was ticking in his cheek.

Carl went on in a low dead voice: "They'll break you, Agnes. They can't let you stand against them. And let me tell you, they've cracked tougher nuts than you. You're not bad—to them you're just a nuisance. They'll wear you down without even thinking about it. To them it'll just be a job."

Agnes's face was smooth and empty now. He turned to Billy. "This old freak thinks we're all going to end up like him— fifty years old and still laying on his back in jail. He must like it here."

He turned and walked to the cell door. "Come on, Billy, I've had about enough preaching."

Billy followed him out. Doug sat up. They hadn't asked him, but he wanted to go with them. But then Carl started talking to him and he couldn't just walk away in the middle of it.

"You don't want to get in with those kids," Carl told him.

"They're OK."

"No, they aren't. They'll just get you into trouble, and you've got enough trouble now."

"I'll be OK," he told Carl. "I think I'll just go out and look around."

He stood up as he said this and he saw Carl digging under the end of his mattress.

"Here, you better have some candy. I know those beans didn't do much for you. Go on. Take it."

Carl held the bar out, with that same look on his face, and Doug couldn't push his hand away. "I'm not really hungry," he said.

"Save it then. Eat it after awhile. There's no string on it, Doug. I've got a whole box. If you get hungry, you just ask me. Will you do that?" The candy bar seemed pathetic. Doug took it and stuck it under his blankets.

"I'll eat it after awhile—when I come back."

He found Agnes and Billy sparring at the end of the tank. They were shuffling around each other, throwing short punches to the body, weaving and snorting through their noses like old-time pugs. Billy had the reach on Agnes, but he didn't know how to use it. He fought in a sideways crouch as if he were afraid of getting hit, and he kept heeling off to the right so he was never set to use his right hand. Agnes shifted from foot to foot, moving in steadily. He didn't move around a lot or try anything fancy, but there was a conciseness to his punching that was pretty to watch. They were both sweating. Doug knew they were just playing, but from the slap of the punches landing, he guessed they weren't holding much back.

Billy gave up first. Dropping his hands, he leaned against the bars, breathing hard. The white skin over his ribs was welted with red patches. Agnes continued shuffling around, snapping punches at the air. Billy wiped the sweat off his forehead with the back of his hand. "Where do you get all the energy?" he asked Agnes.

Agnes shot a classic one-two at his imaginary opponent, and grinned. "Clean living, I guess. It's been three weeks since I took a drink or messed around with a woman. I feel great. Another week of it'll probably kill me." He smiled sideways at Doug. "I'm going to get Sprout here to tell me what it's like. I've damn near forgotten."

Doug liked to see Agnes smile. His teeth were large and white and so even they seemed like a solid band of glistening bone. They transformed his sullen handsomeness into a look of vivid good humor.

He danced up to Doug, hooking a sham left at his head. "Did you get any recently?"

"Not too recently. I've been traveling." To cover his ignorance of that whole subject, Doug threw his hand up, blocking Agnes's left. He cocked his other fist.

"You want to go?" Agnes asked. "Come on—"

Doug pulled his chin in and tried a tentative right.

"Lefty, huh?" Agnes shifted his style, standing square, and the next time Doug tried his right lead, Agnes crossed under it to the solar plexus.

Doug doubled over, breathing in short gasps. He couldn't seem to get any air down. He felt Agnes shaking his shoulder.

"I'm sorry, kid—I didn't mean to hit you so hard. Are you hurt?"

Doug straightened up and managed to get some kind of a smile on his face. He shook his head because he didn't think he could talk without croaking. His diaphragm felt paralyzed.

Billy said, "That Agnes hits like a goddamn mule."

"He wasn't set, that's all." Agnes sounded uncomfortable. "You've got to tighten up," he told Doug. He ridged the muscles of his abdomen and struck himself sharply. "See? Go on. Hit me."

Doug wasn't ready to hit anything, so Agnes turned to Billy. "Come on, Billy, show him."

Billy punched Agnes in the stomach, but he didn't put much shoulder into it. Agnes just grunted.

"See? Nothing to it. You've got to be set, that's all."

Doug was breathing normally again, but he didn't feel like sparring any more. Agnes wiped the sweat off his arms and chest and combed his hair. They settled down, leaning against the bars. Some kind of a march was coming from the television—sounded like a distant parade and it made Doug feel melancholy. Agnes whistled along with it. An old man wandered by in front of them. He was scratching under his arm, and his face was irritable and morose like an old dog's who hasn't felt like chasing anything for years. He dropped the charred stub of a brown-paper cigarette. Billy reached out and crushed it with his foot.

"I wish we had something to smoke," Agnes complained. "This is the hungriest and broke-est jail I ever seen."

"You talk like you'd seen a hundred of them," Billy said.

"I feel like I have. It seems like I've been in here all my life. This your first time?" Agnes asked Doug.

"Not really. I've been in, but not around here."

"You don't act much like it."

"I can't help that. I have been. Lots of times."

"Yeah?" Agnes made it obvious that he didn't believe him, and Doug felt like a fool. He knew he told silly lies that no one would believe, but he couldn't stop telling them.

"What kind of jobs you pull?" Agnes asked.

"Oh, burglaries, mostly."

"Around here?"

"Sure, all over. I travel a lot. I've pulled them all over."

"Yeah?" Agnes leaned towards him, his face serious with interest. "What about this town here? Did you pull many here?"

"Sure. I always do. Anywhere I go."

"But what did you do here? I mean, how was it around here? We weren't here a hot minute before they bagged us."

Doug floundered for a moment, remembering that he didn't know anything about Ardilla either, but then he recalled the list that Terrel had led him through, and he started reciting from it. Both Billy and Agnes listened closely, and Doug experienced a thrill of pleasure. Deep in his mind a clever little chant was going on. "They don't know—they don't know."

Agnes interrupted. "What'd you get out of places like that?"

"Hundreds sometimes."

"That much?" Billy asked with an inflection of doubt.

"Sure, that's nothing."

Agnes shook his head at Billy. "You know what, buddy? Maybe we've been jumping the wrong stump."

Billy made a neutral gesture, but he shifted around to sit out in front of Agnes and Doug. He squatted with his arms resting on his sharp knees.

"Billy and me never thought of anything but sticking a gun in someone's face. That's all we pulled back home, so we thought it'd work out here. But it's a lot different. The country's not built up much, you stick out like a fly on a wedding cake. If they see you around and they don't know you, right away they figure you're a wrongdoer. This thing of yours, you do that mostly at night?"

"Night's the best time," Doug said.

"Well, if we wanted to try it, is there anything special we'd have to know?"

Doug lowered his voice and began to tell them what he'd learned to look for, the little tricks he'd invented, and for almost the first time in his life someone seemed to be really interested in what he had to say, to respect his judgment. But Agnes wasn't as interested in details as he was in money. He broke in again.

"But you find a lot of money?"

"Sure. More than I could spend. I had to hide a lot of it."

"Here in town?"

"Sure. I don't live here, you know. I didn't want to have a lot of money on me. Good thing I hid it, too."

The money was beginning to seem real to Doug. Just talking about it made him feel the same as if he really had it.

"That was pretty smart," Agnes was saying. "You must be pretty smart. I know we never had that much sense. Do you think they'll turn you loose?"

"Sure. I guess they can't hold me if they can't prove nothing on me."

"That's right. Then I guess you'll get that money and light out." Agnes was prompting him, and Doug nodded, smiling securely. He felt their interest beating around him.

Billy was looking hard at Agnes, his eyes shadowed slate-gray and pointed with some message. Doug hardly noticed. He was like a starved dog under a friendly hand, painfully eager and thoughtless.

Agnes caught Billy's eyes and shook his head slightly, his face flexing in a brief negative warning.

"How much you got?" Agnes asked.

"I don't know…." A set figure wouldn't solidify. He rejected one absurdly high figure, and ended up vaguely, "Quite a bit."

"Uh-huh… uh-huh…" Agnes murmured, drawing his lower lip in under his smooth teeth, his eyes vacant. "Well, you did a smart thing."

Agnes got off talking about girls. He related a couple of detailed scenes, and Doug felt his mouth drying up. He held his face in what he thought was a knowledgeable look, and tried to recall some of the other stories he'd heard so he could repeat them as his own experiences. He had no stories of his own. The closest he'd ever come was with a neighbor girl, a thin bony girl; she taught him to kiss her in different ways, but when he'd put his hands on her flat chest, she'd pulled away, looking scared. He didn't try to persuade her, maybe because he was a little scared himself. Still he felt crippled without this special knowledge, as if he were only half a person.

A lock rattling drew their attention. Agnes paused in the middle of an exclamation, and as they looked up they saw three jailers walk into the outside corridor. The music from the television cut off and there was a frozen pause while the hard heels clicked on the concrete. Then the loudspeaker started:

"Lock up! Everyone lock up!"

"Now what?" Billy asked.

"Games," Agnes said mockingly. "We're going to play Cops and Robbers."

"Everyone lock up in their own cells…."

As soon as the cell door slammed, the heat seemed to increase. Doug flopped on his bunk and a puff of hot dust rose from the thick blankets.

"What's up?" Carl asked.

No one answered him. The whole tank was still until the main door rumbled open and they heard the boots of the jailers inside the tank. To Doug it was a bad sound—it reminded him of the gun exploding behind him, and he felt a shiver below his curiosity.

"Sounds like a shakedown," Billy remarked.

Agnes walked to the front of the cell and cocked his head,

listening. The tight frown on his face reminded Doug of how Agnes had looked the night before, peering angrily in the matchlight, as if he had anger enough and guts enough to handle anything. Doug relaxed a little.

"They're not opening the cells," Agnes reported. His frown deepened. "It's something about cups."

"Cups?" Carl repeated. "That's what was used in that cutting this morning—a split-open cup."

"I thought you said nothing would happen," Billy reminded him.

"I'd have bet on it."

The jailers were at the cell next door and Doug heard one of them say, "All right, let's see your cups. Hold them up."

"I guess they want to count cups," Agnes said. "They got nothing better to do." He went to the head of his bed, where his cup was hanging on a piece of bent wire. He lifted it off and slapped it into his hand.

Carl and Billy were getting their cups, so Doug leaned over and brushed his hand under his bunk—he'd shoved his cup there to get it out of the way, but it wasn't in the same place. He lifted his mattress up and looked through the springs, but there wasn't anything on the floor under his bunk except the cardboard center out of a roll of toilet paper and some grayish fuzz.

"Did you see my cup?" he asked Carl.

"Where'd you put it?"

"Right under here, I—"

"All right, let's see your cups."

Doug turned reluctantly.

There were two deputies at the bars. They had their uniform coats off and their khaki shirts were open at the neck. One of them had small metal sergeant's chevrons fixed to his collar.

Agnes, Billy and Carl all held up cups.

"Where's yours?" the sergeant asked.

"I don't know. I can't find it."

"Well, you better find it."

Doug looked under his bunk again even though he knew it wasn't there. The others were all looking around. Carl raised his own mattress. Doug shook his blankets out, and the forgotten candy bar fell to the floor. He turned to look at Agnes, but Agnes was staring past the jailers, out the far window.

"I guess I lost it," Doug told the sergeant.

"You guess? This is a bad day to be losing cups." He took a step back and yelled, "Seven."

The door jerked and rolled open.

"Come on out of there."

Automatically Doug picked up his jacket. He was used to leaving places, uncertain as to whether he'd be back. Agnes squeezed his arm. "Take it easy, Doug. You just keep your mouth shut, and—"

The sergeant turned to look at Agnes. "Can it," he said, drawing the words out with soft disgust. "You better keep your mouth shut, cowboy, or you'll be right out here with him."

They stood him down by the tank door, where the third jailer was on guard. The other two went back to counting cups.

The tank was strange again. Its personality vanished with the prisoners and nothing was left except the blind eye of the television and the cards scattered like old bloodstains on one of the tables. Behind the bars of the closed cells a few men stared out at him, wondering what he'd done. Doug felt separate again and he didn't like it. He wanted to be back in the cell with Billy and Agnes. It was crazy, but he was beginning to like the tank.

The other jailers came back. Everyone else had a cup, and that meant Armando had one. Doug knew what they were thinking: the torn cup would have to be thrown out, and someone would be without one—why did this have to happen to him? Armando was Agnes's buddy; he remembered Billy saying that, but he still didn't want to make the obvious connection.

They took him back down the metal stairs into the booking room. It was the same. There was the same smell of cigarettes smoked weeks ago mixed with the odor of the rubber matting on the floor. The same contradictory sense of boredom and anxiety—all intensified by the heat. A little fan beat futilely in an open window.

A different man was in charge, an older white-haired man with an indoor face. He wore the same khaki uniform, but instead of boots he had on gray felt carpet slippers. He was leaning back in the swivel chair, peeling an orange. The pulp beneath the glistening rind was as white as exposed bone, and Doug vividly recalled the terrified Mexican face, teeth showing through blood. How could they think he'd do something like that?

They left him standing, while the white-haired man—the sergeant called him Captain—looked him over with the same old look: suspicion gradually thawing into a distant and faintly amused sympathy. Doug didn't want it. He squared his shoulders.

The captain divided his orange into segments and ate it, nodding over the sergeant's brief report, then he wiped his hands on the sides of his pants and turned to Doug.

"That Mex try to get funny with you?"

He bent the word "funny" so Doug couldn't miss the meaning. One of the jailers standing behind him snickered. The captain glared him into silence, but Doug still felt his face filling with embarrassment rising out of some obscure humiliation that his appearance should create such a suggestion. He couldn't answer, but stood hearing the whine of the fan.

The captain read his silence for sullenness, and complained to the sergeant about how all these brats thought they were so damn tough. His words had the worn ring of a familiar complaint, but Doug took confidence from them. It was refreshing to be thought of as tough. He leveled his eyes up to meet the captain's and put his hands in his pockets, already framing snatches of sentences to describe the scene to Agnes—how he hard-assed the captain.

But the captain didn't hard-ass worth a damn. He reduced Doug to a mumble with a series of shrewdly related questions: Where was his cup? Who did he give it to? Who was he protecting? Did he know that the Mexican had described his attacker? That they already knew who it was?

Doug made his mistake after the last question. He muttered something to the effect that if they knew who it was why should he have to tell them

"What?" the captain demanded. "What was that?"

"If you know already, why are you asking me?"

The captain shifted deeper into his chair, took out a handkerchief and wiped his neck. "Smart punk," he said. He turned to the sergeant for confirmation. "Smart punk, huh?"

The sergeant nodded.

"All right, smart punk," the captain murmured, "let's see how tough you really are." He turned back to the sergeant. "See what he thinks of the Hole."

CHAPTER TEN

The Hole was a small cell, bare of any but the most essential features, and it hadn't been cleaned in a long time. The inside of the toilet was stained a deep orange below the waterline and the pipes banged and hissed before a brownish trickle would run in the sink. The only light was a forty-watt bulb, recessed into the ceiling and protected by a grate of woven metal strips. A bare mattress covering half the floor space was so old almost all of the cotton tufts were missing; the few remaining were a dark gray. The single blanket felt greasy. The only other object in the cell was a Gideon Bible. The cover was missing and the pages torn out into the middle of Exodus.

The walls were the original brick of the building, repainted many times, and now almost completely covered with a jumble

of names, dates, and initials, the work of men intent on leaving
their record, as before them more powerful men had caused
mountains of stone to be built in the desert. During the first
few hours, Doug read these brief and sometimes tragic his-
tories. Many of the dates preceded his own birth, and it gave
him an eerie feeling to think of men being in this hole before
he was even born, carving the evidence of their passing into
the submerged brick. *A. Lundgren. Going to hang for something
he never done.* The lettering was as neat and compressed as a
bookkeeper's entry. *THE TUCSON KID* was deeply scored
in large jagged capitals, dwindling off towards the floor as the
carver tired and lost his enthusiasm for immortality.

Doug would have added his own name—he thought of calling himself "The Portland Kid"—but he didn't have anything
to scratch with. He could have used the tongue of his belt
buckle, but the sergeant had taken his belt as well as his shoe-
strings. Afraid he'd hang himself. But that was silly because
there wasn't anything to hang from.

There was nothing to do. He tried walking back and forth,
but his shoes flopped without laces, and even when he kicked
them off he still had to keep his hands in his pockets or his
pants would slip down. He picked up the Bible and stared at
the close print, but the unfamiliar syntax threw him off and
he sailed it into the corner, much the same as he'd thrown his
school books away. What he needed to know wasn't in books,
or if it was, it meant nothing that way.

Later, the door opened and some dinner was shoved in by a
khaki arm, obviously some beans left over from lunch, served
on a paper plate with a tiny wooden picnic fork. After he ate
the beans, he tried to scratch the brick with the fork, but the
wood wore away faster than the wall.

He settled on the mattress with his jacket under his head
and tried to feel sleepy. But he wasn't, so he stared at the light
until his eyes smarted, then when he closed them the inside
of his eyelids would flare with small suns, spinning on velvet
until they looked like the skirts of dancers, hanging feet-down

out of the sky, spinning and blurring into one another; and then shifting and stretching until they became bars of violet light, spread out like the rills of the desert after the sun has just set; thickening and darkening until they caged the vision of his inner eye.

Even before he started running away, Doug's life had been an endless series of moves, always moving to new places, and then in a few months moving on. His father was a heavy-construction worker, and he followed the jobs. Wherever the tunnels were going in, wherever they were building bridges or dams, that's where they lived—sometimes in the country, sometimes in towns or cities.

His earliest memories were tied up with the smell and the feeling of furnished rooms, and the uncertainty of strange neighborhoods where he stood around in the city streets or the dirt lanes formed by tarpaper construction shacks, hoping the other kids would invite him to play their games. He never developed any special skills with which to win friendship or recognition; he played an average game of marbles, stickball, and kick-the-can. When teams were being chosen for baseball or football he was always picked close to the last, just before the little kids and the hopelessly bad players. He was never a secure member of the little neighborhood groups. If there was a quarter to be spent at the fountain, somehow he was left out, as he was left off the lists mothers made up for parties, mostly because they didn't know him too well, and his manner was quiet.

In school it was much the same. He was below-average as a student, not because he was dumb, but because for months at a time he was out of school altogether, and because so many different teachers and methods had filled his mind with a disorganized jumble. He might leave one school just as they were starting long division and enter the next just as they were completing it, and he had to struggle to catch up.

His memories of school were hopelessly linked with the agony of standing before a classroom of judging strangers, while the teacher introduced him and found him a seat. That and the humiliation of handing his father a report card full of Ds and Cs. "Hell, kid, can't you do any better than that? Do you want to end up a construction stiff like me?"

His father's thick hair was permanently ridged by the band inside his metal safety helmet, and while his lower face was weathered red by the sun and the wind, his forehead, protected by the hat brim, was a naked white. He seemed incomplete without a hat. He was that kind of man.

Away from him, Doug could admit that his father worked hard, that he was a good builder, but this admission did nothing to kill the years of bitter envy when he'd wished that his father was a clerk in a store, the same store year after year. Yet he knew that wouldn't have been enough to make up for all the mothers he'd had, not that he'd minded most of them—they came and went too—but the thing he hated was that now he couldn't separate his own mother from all the other images, the women who had minded him, dressed him and scolded him. Their different faces blurred in his mind, and it seemed that if he couldn't separate that one special face, his life would never mean anything. Yet at other times this loss didn't affect him, and he didn't think about it.

For a short time he'd been with a gang of kids who stole bottles for the deposits, taking them from garages or back porches and redeeming them at the local grocery for candy or show money. When his father moved on, going to another job site, Doug took the trick with him, and after awhile he worked off the back porches into the houses, and finally into stores. He never took much money because it frightened him to have it; he took enough for shoes and sodas and second-hand adventure magazines, and sometimes he tried to stand treat, but somehow he didn't do it right because the others didn't change towards him for any longer than it took to gobble up his gifts.

At times he thought he was happiest alone in the night, a nameless shadow. There was a funny kind of power in it, almost like being invisible. He would lay on a roof for hours, resting his chin on the damp tarpaper, watching the car lights and the people moving in the street below him, and then it seemed better to be out of it, an unmoved observer hanging above the city, able to take what he wanted when he wanted it. When he climbed back down to the sidewalk, ready to go home, the contrast was so sharp that he could feel himself shrinking to the world's measure of him—a shy kid who couldn't talk very well or dance very well or do anything very well. He didn't want to be that kid.

He thought he could change by running away, taking his life into his own hands, and after several false starts he'd been able to force himself to the decision in the city of Portland. A bad report card had helped; it was in the books he'd pitched into the gulch. He'd thrown all his former life into that gulch and started off with thirty-five cents and the clothes he had on, sure that he would find a way to make it all different. But he'd only wandered into a deeper isolation—shut off from children and not yet an adult, and without the power to break the walls of his shyness.

Until he entered the jail. . . .

A jailer pulled him out in the morning, and he thought he was going back to the tank until he saw Terrel waiting for him in the booking room. He'd forgotten about the ring and he hated to walk into the booking room and face the position he'd put himself into.

But Terrel told him he was going down to court and he'd better comb his hair. They found him a comb in one of the drawers behind the booking desk, and he ran it through his hair, looking around for Bailey Johnson, but he wasn't there. Doug relaxed. He started to hand the comb back, but the jailer told him to keep it.

The courtroom was on one of the lower floors and it wasn't what Doug had expected from the movie courtrooms he'd seen. It was a narrow bare room like a country meeting hall,

with wooden chairs and sterile white plaster; there were flags
on either side of the judge's bench and a Latin motto painted
on the wall behind it. A few people were sitting in the chairs
and some more were gathered around the bench talking quietly. When the judge came in they put their cigarettes out and
fell silent.

"Arraignment," Terrel told him quietly, but that didn't
mean anything to Doug. They sat down to wait, and he
slumped in his chair, wondering if they'd put him back into
the tank. He wanted to tell Agnes about the captain.

Doug recognized another man from the tank a few rows in
front of them, the tall, dark-haired man who'd been playing
poker. Pesco, Agnes had called him. Doug could only see the
side of his face, but he seemed subdued, and much different
than he had in the tank. When he stood up to approach the
bench, Doug saw that he was handcuffed, and the bailiff
waited until he was in front of the judge before he took the
cuffs off.

Terrel nudged Doug. "Take a good look at that fellow, because if you keep on you'll end up like him. He's got so many
charges against him he couldn't do them all if he lived to be
eight hundred years old."

Pesco had his hands behind his back, rubbing his wrists,
while the judge looked down at him like an angry sparrow.
The judge read the charges and Pesco seemed smaller standing
below him listening, but when the judge was finished, Pesco
cleared his throat and said, "Not guilty."

Terrel shook his head. "There isn't anything you can do for
a guy like that."

But Doug had already made up his mind that he was going
to enter the same plea—not guilty.

He wasn't given the chance. The judge wouldn't accept a
plea from him until he'd been advised by counsel, and after
he'd determined that Doug had no money he assigned him a
public defender. Terrel told him the lawyer would come up
and see him in a day or two.

Back in the booking room he found that the captain had left orders to let him out of the Hole in the morning. While the jailer waited to take him back up to the felony tank, Terrel pulled him aside and warned him about the ring. Terrel put it all on Bailey Johnson, how P.O.'d Johnson would be if Doug didn't come up with the ring and any other stuff he had hidden, and despite what Agnes had told him, Doug was still frightened. He couldn't help it, and nothing he could find to tell himself helped at all. He looked at the floor, shuffled his feet and said, "Yes, sir," letting Terrel think that he was ready to do whatever they wanted. And what would he tell them tomorrow? Tomorrow it would be much worse. But maybe they wouldn't come. Even as he thought that, he knew he was lying to himself.

But Terrel was pleased. He brought a quarter out of his pocket. "Here. Buy yourself something to eat when the commissary comes."

Agnes was up; Doug saw him as he entered the tank, lounging against the bars, combing his hair and talking to Pesco. Agnes hailed him. "Hey, buddy!" Grinning and coming towards him. Pesco turned and looked out through the bars towards the window, frowning.

"Damn, buddy, you had me worried. What'd you do? Make the Hole?"

Agnes had a towel around his neck and he was barefoot. His hair was still damp from a shower. Doug sensed that Agnes was more glad than relieved to see him, and he smiled back.

"That's right. I was in the Hole."

"You must have talked pretty sassy to that old captain."

"I didn't tell him anything. I know that much."

Agnes laughed. "I know damn well you didn't. About an hour after they pulled you out, the gang of them came pounding up the stairs like a bunch of hippos. They went through things some, but they didn't find anything."

"I didn't tell him anything."

"I know you didn't, buddy-loo, Pesco tells me they had you down at court."

"It was nothing. Something about an arraignment. But all they did was give me a lawyer."

Agnes dropped back a step and looked at him, studying, his blue eyes full of something like thought. He adjusted the towel on his neck as if it were a scarf. Doug felt a wash of misery, certain that Agnes had penetrated his lies.

But Agnes just punched him on the forearm with the side of his fist, lightly, a friendly gesture.

"That don't look too good. They must think they have you solid. Maybe you left fingerprints or something. Did you think of that?"

"No. Maybe it was fingerprints."

Agnes looked solemn. "Fingerprints are just like leaving your name for them to find."

"It was probably my fingerprints."

"Yeah." Agnes punched him again. "Let's walk."

They went back and forth between the poker game and the tank door, back and forth in the thick air and the solid hard light of the tank, passing the same faces looking out of the empty cream walls. Doug saw Carl watching him from the doorway of their cell, but he pretended not to notice.

Agnes was leading up to something, and Doug was content to let him talk. He noticed with surprise that he was taller than Agnes; he was looking down into Agnes's face, and there was nothing in Agnes's eyes but friendship and a growing excitement. He began to whisper.

"You know what we're planning? Well, I talked to Billy, and we'd like to have you along, but we didn't think you were in enough trouble to have to go that rawjaw, but the way it looks—Well, what do you think?"

It took Doug strangely. He couldn't imagine why they'd want him. "When are you going to try it?" he asked.

Agnes waited until another man walked past them, then he whispered, "Maybe tonight."

So soon. Doug's belly was icy with the thought, but then he realized that if Agnes said they could make it, they could. All he had to do was say yes. He saw a sudden blurred picture of himself and Agnes—maybe even Billy—traveling around the country, stealing what they needed. It would be fine. Terrel could whistle for that ring, and he would never see Bailey Johnson again. He wouldn't have Carl looking at him in that funny way.

He said, "Sure, I'll be glad to go."

Agnes shook his hand. "I knew you'd go for it." He ran to the cell, and Billy came out, rubbing the side of his face. He smiled at Doug too, when Agnes told him. "The more the merrier," he said. "It's your secret too, now."

"We didn't have to worry about him. You got a right to go, Doug. You're helping to pay for the blades. I didn't know who you were then. You know what I mean?"

Doug knew Agnes was talking about his watch, but that didn't matter now. He didn't need it.

They settled down in a corner and began to talk plans, and Doug felt the excitement squeezing out of him; he shifted his feet and banged his hands together and he wanted to laugh out loud, or shout or something.

Agnes laid it out: Slim was going to bring the blades at noon, and they'd saw out that night. Agnes paused and touched Doug on the arm. "We'll handle all that, but after we get out then you can take over. We're going to need some money fast, from somewhere right here in town, and—"

Doug continued to nod his head, but he couldn't keep smiling. It didn't surprise him that that was the reason they wanted him—he should have expected it—but it was just that he wished he really had some money. He didn't mind them wanting it, only now they would find him out for sure. He started smiling again, feeling like a phony.

When the tempo of the talk died down, Doug asked Agnes what he thought had happened to his cup. Agnes shrugged. "Damned if I know, buddy."

CHAPTER ELEVEN

Slim was having trouble making up his mind. He spent some of the morning laying on his bunk in the trusty dormitory. In Slim's mind the whole jail was laid out as precisely as a floor plan, because he'd tried to devise an escape of his own and abandoned it as hopeless. Now he tried to guess what Agnes had in mind, wondering if Agnes had found something he had overlooked. There were sometimes holes so obvious that no one thought of them. Slim remembered the jail they'd put up in Kansas. For six months they'd boasted about how escape-proof it was going to be, and yet the very week they'd opened it someone had wandered out with as much effort as it took to go down to the corner for a beer. Remembering this, Slim had some second thoughts about Agnes. He thought of the two metal doors between the booking room and the tank. There was no way through them, and even if there were, they wouldn't have a chance to make it onto the elevator, and that was the only way down from the jail. Even in the tank itself it seemed hopeless, because if they could manage to get out, they still had the bars to saw out of the window, and the patrol would pick them up before they could get started. No. He didn't have to worry about them making it.

But somewhere there was profit to be turned in Agnes, if only the watch and the cigarettes, which Slim couldn't discount because of his debts. But he had a larger reason gnawing at him, an endless leaking of anxiety.

He had a hold. When his county time was completed he wouldn't be freed, but turned over to the officers of his own state, to be handcuffed and shackled and taken down the elevator and out into a transportation vehicle. He wouldn't even see the city. He'd be locked in, and when he stepped out he'd be back inside the walls, just as if they'd led him through a long tunnel from one jail into another.

He didn't want to go back—with an intensity that amounted

to anguish. The whole process seemed so mechanical, as if where caught in the wheels of a vast machine that there was no way to turn off, and yet he had to keep trying to turn it off. In his mind he worried it with a desperate and futile energy, turning everything in the light of this single purpose, and Agnes had suggested a plan to him, a plan so contrary to his primary convictions that it gagged him like the thought of incest.

But what was Agnes? Agnes was nothing. A brainless punk who thought it was smart to mimic the men Slim truly admired—the men who struck the flames and fell burning, the last of the old hardheads who truly didn't give a damn. Agnes was just saying the same words, striking attitudes he wasn't man enough to live out. Giving Agnes hacksaw blades would be like giving a kid a water pistol and letting him play it was a real gun. Agnes wouldn't be able to do anything with the blades except jump around and wave them in people's faces, the same as saying, Look what I got! He'd make a lot of noise to impress his punk friends, heat the whole jail up, and end up getting caught. That was sure. He would be caught anyway.

Slim stood up and walked over to where his working mate Corky was sleeping. Slim stared down at Corky, his thin sharp face drawn with contempt. Corky was a snitch, and Slim hated to work with him. But now it was going to pay off.

Might as well get it over with, he told himself, before this little jerk wakes up and queers the whole deal. He went down the central corridor and entered the booking office. He lied to the captain, telling him Corky was sick, and managed to get a pass down to the lower floors to pick up the spittoons for cleaning, a job Corky usually handled.

Five minutes later he stood in the dim quiet of the police garage arguing with the trusty mechanic, the mechanic was afraid the blades might be traced to him, but he wanted the split Slim was offering him. They struck a compromise. The blades he gave Slim were worn out, discarded by some previous mechanic, probably unrecorded and certainly nearly useless.

He pulled them out of the scrap box, and handed them to Slim, warning him, "These aren't much good."

Slim smiled. "I don't care if they wouldn't cut hot butter."

CHAPTER TWELVE

Agnes was on Slim as soon as he stepped into the outside corridor. He waved Billy and Doug back, following Slim along the bars like a coyote following a sheep on the other side of a fence, pacing him, hungry but impotent. He watched impatiently while Corky and the jailer Zack started the feeding.

When he caught Slim's eyes, he instantly sensed the difference in Slim's face and his heart began to pound. We made it, he thought wildly, we goddam well made it! He wanted to shout and kick the other men out of his way so he could get at Slim. He got his chow and ran to the cell for his cup, thinking over and over: This is it.

But when he caught Slim down at the quiet end of the tank, Slim's face had changed again. It was gray and guarded, flat-eyed, looking down at him. Agnes put his cup against the bars and whispered, "You made it, didn't you?"

"Take it easy," Slim cautioned. "You'll give the whole deal away. Have you got the watch and the smokes?"

"Sure."

"Have them ready this afternoon. I conned the regular man into letting me mop up."

Slim quickly poured his coffee and moved on. For a moment Agnes stared after him, vaguely uneasy. Then the excitement hit him all at once, and he rushed off to look for Armando.

He found him sitting up in his bunk, watching out the bars. One of Armando's cell partners was in the opposite bunk, so Agnes motioned to Armando. Billy and Doug moved up behind him and he sensed them all looking at him, waiting. He felt a tingle of power and slouched against the bars, feeling his lips curve in a negligent hero's smile.

Armando came over and looked up at him. His face was paling from lack of sunlight, and his eyes had the dull luster of teak.

"What happened, man?" His voice was tight and hard.

Agnes ignored the question and drawled one of his own. "You guys feel like getting out of here?"

"Don't fool around, man. Did you get them?"

Agnes didn't lose his smile. He looked at all three faces, and then said, "No."

Armando began to swear in Spanish.

"But I will this afternoon."

"Is that what he said?" Billy asked eagerly.

"That's it. This afternoon. What do you think of that, Doug?"

"Fine. That's really fine."

Billy reached over and scrubbed Agnes's hair. "I knew you could do it, buddy."

Agnes ducked away, reaching for his comb. Armando was smiling one of his rare smiles; his teeth lit his dark face and his eyes became soft. "You know, man," he said to them all, "I'm going to get so damn far out of this country so damn fast, they be thinking I'm a goddam jet. And once I get over that border—that's it. They can forget about me. I'll be just one more peon."

"That's the way," Agnes agreed, "we'll probably go back home too. We didn't lose nothing out here. Nothing but our freedom."

"We were just going through, anyway," Billy added.

Doug didn't have anything to say. Agnes glanced at him and felt the pleasant weight of Doug's admiration. Let the kid tag along.

Frazier was still upset by what he had overheard. For him it had changed the feeling of the tank just as much as if they had come in the night and painted everything red. Everything he saw and heard glared in a harsher light. Still he tried not to let it interfere with his orderly habits, and one of these was to take a certain amount of exercise each day. He walked briskly up and down the tank, counting off the trips, going what he had worked out to be approximately a mile. This seemed a good distance to walk, and it had the virtue of being definite.

Now he stepped out of his cell and turned towards the television, wading into a rising storm of organ music. He turned short of the men seated Indian-fashion around the screen and headed back the other way, keeping as far clear of the poker game as he could. He walked with his hands behind him and his head down like an admiral or a board member, and he was almost past Agnes and the others before he noticed them. Then some impulse forced his head up and to the side—he was staring right into Agnes's eyes. He experienced a shock, almost like recognition, and he smelled the tension in the group as an animal would. He betrayed his awareness by looking away too quickly and hurrying on to the other end of the tank. He pretended to be looking out the round window in the tank door, staring at the farther door that led down into the booking room, but he was seeing Agnes and the Mexican, and his mind was mushy with anxiety.

He turned back. Agnes was still looking after him, he caught the weight of Agnes's eyes, as hard and bright as blue stones, and he ducked his head and plunged back past the group.

He couldn't keep from pausing in the door of his own cell to take one more look, hoping somehow their attitude would suddenly seem innocent. Agnes was still watching him.

He gave up any idea of exercising, and climbed awkwardly into his bunk. As he lay listening to Tharp's clogged respiration, he had a sudden stinging impulse to bash Tharp in the nose in the hope of plugging it up altogether. The very impulse surprised him just as much as if he had yielded to it.

Agnes nudged Billy. "Did you see that clown?"
"The one with the necktie?"

"Yeah."

"Who?" asked Armando.

"He just went by. An old guy with a necktie. Do you think he was trying to get an earful?"

"He was just walking," Billy said, not very interested. "He's some kind of exercise freak—he goes trotting back and forth every day."

"I know that, but I still think he acted funny. And that's not half of it. I think he overheard me when I was talking to Slim yesterday. He was sitting right there."

Armando scowled. "Why don't you be more careful?"

Agnes flared under the criticism. "How'd I know he was there? He's one of those creepy bastards you never pay any attention to."

"We'd better pay some attention to him now. We're too close to be fooling around," Billy said gravely. "We'd better watch him."

"I'll watch him," Armando volunteered, staring thoughtfully down the line of cells.

"We'll all watch," Agnes said with decision, taking back the initiative. "The first phony move he makes, we'll jump him, and put him out until after tonight."

Armando went back to his own cell to finish eating, and Billy and Doug and Agnes all went down to their end of the tank.

After they ate, they sat around on the concrete and tried to find ways to dilute their nervousness. Agnes didn't like waiting for something—that was the worst of it for him. Every time something rattled outside the tank, he jumped up and ran down to the door.

It was mid-afternoon before Slim finally came.

"Get the stuff," Agnes told Billy.

He stood watching as Zack let Slim into the outside corridor. Slim backed in, carrying a mop and a bucket of gray water. Agnes could smell the disinfectant from where he was standing.

Zack looked the tank over with a jailer's habitual examination, and Agnes turned away quickly so Zack couldn't see his face and read any special tension there.

He walked to the end of the tank and pretended to watch television, straining for the sound of the gate closing over the meaningless noise from the set. Someone he knew slightly slapped him on the back. "How's it going, Agnes?"

Agnes almost hit him.

When the gate sounded, he started back. Zack was gone, and Slim was already sloshing the mop around. He rushed towards Slim, making a big casual show in case anyone was watching.

"Hey! Old buddy! Well, look at that. They finally got you a job you can handle."

His voice was too loud, and he heard its phony ring. Slim glared at him, slapping the mop on the floor.

"Tom's sick," Slim said for whoever might be listening. Then, lower, "Take it easy."

"You got them?" Agnes asked.

"You got the cigarettes?" Slim countered.

"They're in the cell."

"Get them."

"How you going to carry them?"

"Let me worry about that."

Agnes hurried to the cell. Billy had the cigarettes ready, wrapped in an old newspaper. "Get the blades first," Billy whispered.

"Think I'm a fool?"

Slim was working along, swinging the mop carelessly. Agnes caught him in a quiet area between the game and the television. He shoved Slim the package and said, "Let's see them."

Slim bent down and pretended to be adjusting the clamp on the mop. He pulled a slender strip of folded and taped paper out of his sock, and dropped it on the floor; then he stood up and kicked it under the bars.

Agnes flexed it and felt the tiny teeth through the paper.

He grinned: "Goddam, old buddy, you're all right."

"Just give me the smokes."

Agnes unwrapped the cigarettes and fed them through the bars, a carton at a time. Slim hid them: two in back of his belt, and one under his arm. He didn't look much different when the cigarettes had disappeared.

Agnes handed him the watch and he bounced it in his palm. "OK. Take it easy."

Slim hastily spread water over the dry parts of the floor and went up and rattled the gate. Zack let him out.

"That was fast enough."

Slim chuckled. "I'm hell with a mop."

Agnes stood listening, feeling the edge of the hacksaw gripped tightly in his palm, thinking, We made it! The others gathered around him and he got Billy by the arm, and shook him, shouting into his face, "We made it, buddy, we made it!" And he felt like a hunter who brings meat after a long hungry spell.

Billy said, "Let's take a look at them."

Agnes surrendered his prize and Billy unwrapped it, shielding what he was doing with his body. Armando and Doug drew closer. Agnes saw the broken end and he said softly, "That mother fucker."

"What's wrong?" Armando demanded.

"These are used," Billy said. He was looking at the blades carefully, trying to hold them in the light and still keep them hidden. "They might make it," he decided in a cautious voice. "It'll be close, but they might make it."

"Get off it," Agnes snarled in bitter contempt. "You think these snitches are going to let us saw and saw for two or three days? The first time they get out, one of them will sell us for an extra slice of bread. You know that."

"Look, man, what're you talking about?" Armando's voice was screwed down to a flat murmur, his eyes bleak.

Billy said, "These blades are old and they'll take longer to cut. Once we start sawing, everyone in the tank's going to know it. If we can't saw through tonight, tomorrow when they start pulling guys out of here, one of them'll split on us, sure as you're born. They'll bust in here and find us half-finished. You see?"

Armando saw. They all looked around uneasily. The others. Which one would tell? Or more likely, which one would get to the jailers first? Frazier wasn't in sight, but Agnes thought of him. Frazier had become the symbol of that fear.

Billy faced Agnes squarely. "I'm telling you, these'll probably make it."

"Look, don't fool around." Armando stared up at Billy, more Indian than Spaniard in his face. "Will those get us out?"

Billy hesitated. He looked at the blades again, feeling the tooth with his thumb. "I know tools," he said. "These'll make hard work of it, but they'll do the job. I don't know if they'll do it in time. It's a gamble."

"OK," Armando decided. "We'll try it."

Agnes stared at Armando, wondering if he thought he was just going to take over. Armando turned to him, matching his eyes. "You don't like it, man?" he inquired softly.

"Okay, buddy, take it easy," Agnes said, flushing as much from the need for caution as from anger. "If you're so tough why didn't you chew your way out?"

Armando hit him—a chopping blow that caught him on the ear. And at the same time Armando aimed a kick at his groin. Agnes covered, and Billy jumped between them, throwing Armando to the side.

"Lay off!"

Agnes felt Doug's arm clamped around his chest, and beneath the buzzing in his ear he heard Billy saying, "Take it easy. Take it easy. You'll bring heat." Billy was facing him, his arms stretched out, moving from side to side, trying to hold Armando away.

Agnes wrenched free. "Better get away, Billy," he sobbed. "I mean it. Out of my way." His head pulsed and his stomach felt like it was on fire.

Billy grabbed him around the arms, almost like an embrace. Billy's face right up to his, white and shouting, "Ernie! These'll work! Goddammit, Ernie, you know what this means? We'll be going home!"

His true name stopped him. It was Billy's claim to their old friendship, his way of telling him how much this meant to them. He quieted and looked over Billy's shoulder. Armando was still too, rubbing the back of his hand on his mouth. He looked up at Agnes and his eyes were human again, grave and simple.

"I'm sorry, man. I'm all hopped up. I feel bad, no kidding. You want to punch me in the mouth—go ahead."

Agnes smiled slightly. "It was my ear. I can still feel it."

"The ear, anything. It's OK, man."

"It's all right, buddy. If you hadn't hit me, I'd of probably hit you." Agnes was still smiling, even as he went on thinking. But if I did hit you it wouldn't be in the nuts. If you had to hit your friends you didn't try to kick them there. He knew he'd never feel right with Armando again, but it didn't matter. That was the great part—it didn't matter.

He turned to Billy. "Can we start after sick call and be out tonight?"

Billy said, "Sick call's about five, and they lock the cells at nine. That's four hours."

"We got to have at least an hour's start, before they count at lock-up."

"Three hours to saw. Damn it, I don't know. I think so."

"That's it then," Agnes said with decision. "We've got to chance it."

CHAPTER THIRTEEN

Doug couldn't resist the thrill of partnership. It didn't matter
that his share was small; it didn't even matter that it was false.
He found ways to forget the falseness. The money was easy to
get out of. He would pretend he was leading them somewhere,
and when he found a likely spot he'd stop and look. The money
would be gone. Someone would have found it.

It didn't matter. He was sure he could get money some other
way.

"Did you ever see anything so pretty?" Agnes asked, holding
the blades so Carl couldn't see them. Doug caught the flicker
of interest in Carl's eyes: he was lumped in his bed with his
pants open at the top to ease his belly. Twice since he'd come
back to the tank, Carl had tried to get him alone to talk with
him, but he was always with Billy and Agnes now and that
was the way it was going to be.

"Come on," Agnes whispered, "I'll show you how we're
going to make it."

He slipped the blades to Billy in the cover of his towel.

"Be careful," Billy cautioned.

But Agnes shook it off, smiling at Doug as if Billy was an
old woman.

"Come on."

Doug followed, full of Agnes's mood, a harsh excitement
hidden by a pose of casual daring. They drifted up to the middle of the tank. Agnes paused to trade insults with Pesco and
moved on to drink from the sink. He teetered on his heels, his
mouth pursed in an empty whistle.

No one was paying any attention. Agnes stepped back and
pulled open the canvas shower curtain. It was heavy with
water and stained with rust. The inside of the shower was
painted the same uniform gray as the rest of the tank, and a
large watering-can nozzle pointed down. The nozzle leaked
steadily and the walls were wet.

"In here?" Doug asked, bewildered.

"Why do you think I take so many showers? I ain't that clean."

Agnes motioned him inside and let the curtain fall closed behind them. A line of rivets went up the center of the back wall, and a little above eye-level the line was broken by a spot of light. Agnes stood on his tiptoes and put his eye to the hole left by the missing rivet. He smiled like a child rediscovering a favorite toy. "Now that's something. Our ticket home."

Agnes dropped down and stepped back, inviting Doug to look.

Doug pressed his face against the wet wall, closing one eye. He was looking into a narrow area full of pipes and dust, a passageway of some kind. Directly across from his line of vision, about three feet away, was an unbarred window, slightly open at the top, containing a bird's nest and a spider web, silvered in the light.

"Look down," Agnes told him.

He saw that the shower was recessed in such a way that he could see the back of one of the tank walls, and near the bottom that wall was ruptured by a ragged hole, about a foot across.

"Where's that?" he asked Agnes.

Agnes grinned and posed. "Isn't that something?"

They stepped out of the shower and in the corner beyond the sink, Agnes moved aside a pile of scrub brushes and two mop buckets, uncovering a square slab of metal patched on the wall.

"There must have been a can or something here. Whatever it was, they ripped it out and welded this patch on. It must have been some time ago—see where it's beginning to rust?" He scraped some of the scale away from the old welding scar. He looked up at Doug, quiet and serious, and Doug began to believe in the reality of the escape.

"We can start at this corner, and once we get going we can saw the weld right out. Underneath is that hole you saw. We'll go through it and right out that window. And that's it."

Doug remembered the window, dusty and untouched like the window of a vacant house.

"What's back there?" he asked.

"The plumbing. Wires and stuff. They must have figured no one would ever get back in there, because they didn't even bar those windows."

"How are we going to get down from the window?"

"That's nothing. We'll make a rope out of blankets."

"Isn't this the fifth floor?"

"Sure. We'll make a long rope." Agnes laughed and shuffled around Doug, throwing sham punches. "Well? What do you think? Huh? How do you like it?"

"I'm glad you asked me along."

"Hell, there ain't no limit—not as far as I'm concerned. I hope they all go. Can't you see their faces when they come in to count and there isn't a mother's son left in here? We'll even shove old Carl through. You think he won't be a tight fit?"

"Is he going?" Doug asked uneasily.

"Hell, no. You couldn't run Carl out of here with a shotgun. He likes it here."

Billy came up, rolling his sleeves and smiling, but it was obvious that he was nervous. Agnes questioned him sharply about the blades.

"They're under my mattress."

"What about Carl?"

"He's sleeping." Billy turned to Doug. "Think that'll work?"

"Billy found it," Agnes said carefully.

Doug was flattered, even though he sensed that Billy just wanted to hear what a fine idea it was all over again. "Sure, it'll work," Doug told him seriously. "How'd you ever find it?"

"I knew there had to be some out. I just kept looking."

"We're practically home," Agnes announced, leaning back against the sink, and Doug saw his eyes leave the present and drift away.

"You going home?" Doug asked quietly.

"Quick as we can get."

"We'll be safe back home," Billy added. Then after a moment's silence. "You know what, Ernie? I think maybe I'll take that job with Pot and Harry."

Doug felt them slide away into all the things they had been before, the bond between them laced by so many common memories. Where would he go when they went home? It occurred to him that they'd probably let him go along, but it seemed, like all his wishes, a way to ease the weight of truth. He knew what would happen. They wouldn't throw rocks at him, but he wouldn't fit where they belonged. For a moment he thought of staying behind in the jail, hard as it would be to back out, but as he tried to think ahead into what that future might be, he saw himself alone with Carl, without Agnes between them, and he saw Terrel and Bailey Johnson coming for him.

Doug heard a new voice and turned to see Armando sitting on the other side of Billy. He felt a little strained because he had never said anything to Armando and he didn't know what the Mexican thought of him. There was a quiet in Armando's face as if the things he thought might be much different from his expression, but Doug didn't know. He just didn't like to feel awkward.

He kept thinking of the night coming outside, and the rope stretching down five stories, and the gun going off behind him that first night in the feed store.

The television turned into a clock and every time the program changed, Agnes would mark it. "Four o'clock. Only another hour."

When Frazier came out to take a shower he saw the four boys sitting along the bars. None of them looked more than a few years out of school, but there they were crouched there like animals. Where'd that boy come from? Frazier wondered of Doug. He really looks like he should be in school. Something's wrong when a boy like that.... Agnes's hard blue eyes drove Frazier back into his own concerns.

He fumbled the wrapper off of his soap and threw his dirty
underwear on the shower floor. He was intensely self-con-
scious as he began to undress. He looked down at his body,
and it seemed white and powerless. He was glad to get in the
shower and hide himself with the curtain.

"That bastard's getting on my nerves," Agnes complained
to Armando. He didn't know just when he'd decided, or even
how, but he was convinced that Frazier was a rat.

"What's he doing in there?" Armando asked. The shower
had come to seem like their personal place.

"Snooping around. He's going to find something he ain't
looking for."

Armando shifted on his heels, looking along their faces,
then back to where the water was pattering on the shower
curtain. He didn't say anything more. His hands hung relaxed
between his legs.

Dinner came. The food seemed even more tasteless than
usual. Agnes dumped his out, but Billy and Doug tried to
eat.

"You ought to eat," Billy told Agnes. "You don't know when
you'll get another chance."

But Agnes wouldn't listen. He kept running over to look
out the window in the door, or going back to check on the
shower. Armando ate just as if it were any other night.

After dinner sick call was held; anyone who needed medicine
filed down into the booking room where a small dispensary
was kept. Agnes was alert to see if Frazier would go out. All
he had to worry about now was Frazier, and even when Frazier
wasn't in the line Agnes wasn't satisfied. He hurried along
the cells until he found Frazier in his bunk. You just stay there,
he thought.

Sick call straggled back in. Finally the door banged, and
they heard the jolting of the levers. Agnes ran to the tank door

FELONY TANK   89

and saw Zack leaving through the door down into the booking office. The door closed behind him.

He ran back. "Get the blades, Billy."

Then Agnes stood quietly, looking up and down. There wasn't anything happening inside of him, except that some instinct within him was reaching out to feel the temper of the tank. He shook his head abruptly, and slammed his fist into his palm.

"Let's try it."

Agnes put Armando up by the tank door as a lookout and motioned for Billy and Doug.

For an instant Doug thought, We shouldn't do this. He sensed something of the complexity of the thing they were setting the teeth of the hacksaw against, and it seemed much better to get in his bunk and read a magazine. But he moved into the job Agnes had assigned him, because that was what the others were doing.

Billy went behind the sink while Agnes and Doug stood in the mouth of the alcove, trying to act casual. In a moment they heard a harsh noise, faltering, trying to take a rhythm and, then starting up again. It was too loud.

"Jesus, Billy, hold it down!"

"I can't. I haven't got room to work."

Agnes rushed back and Billy showed him how there was no clearance for his hand. "But as soon as I've got the corner started, it'll go easier."

Agnes traced the thin line of bright metal in the cut. "It's all right. It's working. We'll cover you."

Agnes started singing *In the Evening by the Moonlight*, motioning to Doug to join in. Doug only knew the first line, but Agnes bellowed on, and after a moment he picked it up. He had to—the sound of the hacksawing frightened him more than he wanted to admit.

"The old folks would enjoy it...." Men turned around from the television to shout, "Dummy up!"

"Dummy your mother up!" Agnes countered. "... as we

sang love's old sweet song...."

Agnes stayed away as long as he could, then he ducked back to peer over Billy's shoulder. "How's it going?"

Billy held his hand up—his knuckles were scraped raw. But Agnes only glanced at it—his eyes were on the cut. It had gone only three—maybe four—inches.

Agnes dug his hand into Billy's shoulder. "You're making it. Goddammit, buddy, you're making it."

CHAPTER FOURTEEN

Agnes won't wait. He hasn't got the patience. He's probably trying to saw right now....

Slim pictured the felony tank as he remembered it from the evening, and he saw the waves of shock moving out from Agnes and the sound of his sawing. He saw the heads turning and heard the tense, frightened whispers, as every man in the tank tried to decide what this was going to mean to him. He could almost hear someone deciding to turn Agnes over. Someone in the tank would make that decision.

Slim smiled, but his stomach hurt, and when he stood up he almost stumbled. He lifted his hair up off his ears and smoothed it around in back of his head.

He had to stand humbly for a moment before the captain would notice him. Ordinarily he would have interrupted the captain's reading, taking a glum joy in an expression of hostility he couldn't be called up on. But his present job rattled him.

What am I supposed to do? he asked himself defensively. It isn't like they had any real chance.

The captain looked up.

"Captain, I wanted to see you for a minute."

The captain didn't ease the weight any, he just swung around in his chair, and Slim realized that the captain didn't see him as a man with problems, but only as some sort of badly made thing.

When Slim sensed this, the old smarting began in him—screw you, Captain, sir; I'm more man than you'll ever be. But his venom didn't heal him this time. He sagged under the necessity of going ahead.

"I got a hold, Cap. I guess you know that."

The captain nodded, and Slim felt a little better for being recognized. Then someone moved behind him and he turned to see Zack come in, swinging his keys in a leather case. "Everything's tight, Cap." Zack leaned against the booking desk and watched him with idle curiosity. Slim hated to go on begging them.

"Mr. Zack," he said, "I was just talking to the Captain."

"Go right ahead," Zack smiled. "Don't mind me, I just work here."

Slim turned to see the captain smiling too, and he had to go into that smile as if he were pushing against a great weight.

"I'm worried about my hold, Cap. I owe them five years, and—well, I just thought that maybe—"

He faltered again, looking for some encouragement in the captain's face; there was nothing there but the beginning of alertness. The captain had caught the scent.

Slim rushed on, getting it over with. "I know about something that's going on. Something pretty serious."

"What?"

"Can't we make some kind of a deal? You've got to help me on that hold. If you wrote and told them I'd really straightened out, I think they'd listen to you. Then they wouldn't come after me."

The captain said, "We'll see."

"You'll help me, won't you, Cap?"

"I said I'd see. Now what's this all about?"

Slim hesitated, but he'd reached the end of his resources. He knew it and the captain knew it.

"There's something going on in the felony tank. I got word of it and I've been keeping my eyes open when I go in there, and now I'm sure of it—"

"What is it?" The captain was sitting up straight, his eyes intense.

Oh, you're interested now, aren't you? Slim thought. He smiled. "They're trying to escape."

"How do you know that?"

"I don't know definite, but I'm sure of it. You can't miss it when you've been around as many of these buckets as I have. You know what I mean?"

The captain nodded. "How are they trying to go?"

"They're sawing out."

"Sawing out?"

"That's right, Cap."

"When?"

"I don't know for sure. Soon, maybe right now." The captain watched him for a moment longer, then he turned his back. "Okay, we'll check on it... and thanks."

Slim knew he was dismissed, but he couldn't leave it as it was. For a moment the hatred in him shifted and found its true object, and he stood in front of the captain, humble and useless, and begging not to be blamed for it.

"You'll help me, won't you?"

"I'll see."

The captain was through with Slim and he made it obvious; he wanted to think about what Slim had told him. But Slim couldn't leave. He needed to hear something he could repeat to himself later, something that could serve as justification to the reproaches that would leak through his anger.

"A letter from you would mean a lot, Cap. They'd listen to you."

The captain leaned back in his chair and really looked at Slim. The half-man demanding pity. The captain thought of the pests he rooted out of his flower garden, the hearty weeds and the slugs that moved along on a river of their own slime. He said slowly and deliberately, "There is a county regulation that prohibits me from writing to another state in your behalf."

"You won't write?"

"I can't. Now get out of here."

In the hall, out of sight, Slim turned and gave the captain the finger, jamming it up into the air with violent, frustrated tension. He was sick with fury, and his fury burned away the details of the incident until he was left with the single realization that they had fucked him again. What can you expect? he asked himself bitterly.

The captain asked Zack, "You notice anything?"

"Nothing much."

"You think there's anything to that?"

Zack smiled. "Like he said, he's got hold."

"Yes, that's what I was thinking, but you'd better check it out."

"All right, but it's probably just talk. You know how they're always talking."

Zack opened the door leading up to the felony tank, and the faint sound of singing came into the room. He paused.

"Listen to that."

"It doesn't have to mean anything." The captain sounded uneasy.

Zack said, "If they *are* trying to cut out, it's going to be hard to catch them at it. By the time I can get the door open they'll have scattered. I'll find the cuts, but not the men."

The captain thought a moment, then said, "If you find anything, don't let on. Just make out like it was your regular round. Maybe we can arrange a little surprise for them."

Zack was concentrating on being quiet on the stairs, so he missed the flash of Armando's head withdrawing behind the window. He tiptoed to the gate of the outside corridor and unlocked it.

The bars were clear the whole length of the tank. No one was near them, except the edge of the crowd around the television. The poker game was going, but there were only a few players. Other men stood in front of their cells, their blurred faces turning to him.

Zack nodded and padded slowly along the bars, trying to inspect them and still not give away what he was doing. No one made him any greeting or asked him anything. That was odd. They were always full of gripes. They looked at him but they didn't say anything, and their faces seemed stiff.

Something was up. He could taste the tension in the air like brass on his tongue. No one was talking in the whole tank, just the unnatural voice of the television.

All right, he thought, what are you up to?

Walking back the other way, he was able to inspect the other side of the bars, but they were whole. The paint wasn't even scratched. Maybe they're just starting.

Closing the gate behind himself, he picked a place along the outside wall where it was impossible for anyone in the tank to see him. He pushed his cap to the back of his head and lit a cigarette. After a couple of drags, he placed his ear to the metal wall.

He heard the distant murmur of the television. That was all, until the singing started again. Then he heard the sawing. He'd never heard anything quite like it before, but he knew instantly what it was. He stepped on his cigarette and moved along the wall.

That's nowhere near the front bars, he decided. What the hell are they trying to pull? He was baffled, but he knew better than to enter the tank again—that would alert them for sure.

Sometimes the sawing seemed distant, sometimes closer, but he couldn't grasp any certain direction, until he noticed the small door into the utility tunnel, and something clicked in his mind.

The utility tunnel ran the full length of the tank in back of all the cells, handling all the pipes and wire. Several times he'd entered it with repairmen and he remembered that the windows in there weren't barred. So they were going that way.

As soon as he had the door open, the sound of the sawing grew louder. He nodded with satisfaction and began to tiptoe down the large central pipe. A small bulb at each end filled the tunnel with shadows, but the sound of the sawing guided Zack until he came to the area behind the shower and the moving end of the saw caught his eye. He watched the saw blade moving sluggishly, and he imagined the man on the other side of the wall. Just a moment ago he'd been working towards freedom, and now? Now he was sawing his way into serious trouble.

Zack shrugged. He had no power to change the rules. He tried to estimate how much longer it would take them to finish the sawing—he could see it was going slowly—and he guessed it would be over an hour.

He tiptoed back up the utility tunnel, eager now to get to the captain. He knew the captain would probably decide to let them go until they were so far into their plans that a conviction for escape would be automatic.

CHAPTER FIFTEEN

Ten minutes after they started sawing, everyone in the tank knew something was wrong. They came out of their cells and looked around carefully, until they saw Agnes in front of the shower—then they suddenly weren't interested. The men watching television couldn't keep their minds on the screen. They heard the singing and the sawing and they knew they would be affected by it. All jails were run to snub the most violent, but the meek were snubbed as harshly, and their fear of change and trouble created the tension Zack had sensed so easily. Doug, too, was sensitive to the intense feeling around him. He'd heard one man mutter, "Those damn kids are going to get us all in trouble." So when Pesco came towards them, scowling, Doug stepped behind Agnes, even though he continued to sing.

Pesco yelled at Agnes, throwing his hands down in a gesture of disgusted impatience. "Jesus! What's that bellowing for?

What the hell are you up to?"

Pesco broke off, looking over Agnes's shoulder into the alcove. His hard face grew quiet, and he asked matter-of-factly,
"You think you can get away with it?"

Doug saw Agnes's familiar grin, pleased and cocky. He broke
off singing to say, "No, we won't make it. Billy just wanted
some exercise."

"You're really at it, aren't you?" Pesco's admiration was obvious and Doug was pleased to be included in it. Agnes took
Pesco into the shower to peek through the hole and a moment
later he was singing with them. Doug knew no one would try
to stop them now. Pesco sang at the top of his voice.

Billy came out, rubbing his hand. His face was pale; his hair
was messed and streaked on his forehead. Blood was trickling
down his fingers and he wiped it on his pants.

"I've got to break," he said, and it sounded like an apology.
"My hand's beginning to cramp."

Agnes avoided looking at the blood still tracing down Billy's
hand. "We've got to keep going," he said stubbornly.

"I'll saw," Doug offered.

It was hard work that very quickly became painful. He tried
to work fast, anxious to get a lot done so Agnes would be
pleased, but the flexible blade bound in the cut, springing out
and causing his knuckles to scrape against the wall. He wasn't
used to working and he couldn't seem to get set for it. The cut
hardly seemed to move forward at all. It didn't seem possible
they'd ever get through.

Then Agnes gripped his shoulder. "That's the way, buddy,
you're moving."

He tried to saw faster. His arm was tired already, but he
couldn't quit or complain. He knew he had to do this until
someone relieved him or he finished the job. After awhile his
arm was numb and his knuckles raw. Every stroke caused him
pain, but he still wouldn't quit.

Then Agnes came in and tried to work, but he was no good
at it and Billy took over again.

Doug stood singing, rubbing his arm. He felt pretty good. He went back and held his hand under the tap. Billy had the patch pried up now, and he was working steadily.

Agnes worried. The programs seemed to speed by on television, the bright dialog sounding like some alien and senseless language, totally without reality. He felt like smashing the machine. They had to hurry.

"Won't it go any faster?" he asked Billy.

"Not with these blades. The damn things were worn out to begin with and they ain't getting any better. Don't worry. We get three sides and I think we can pry it off."

When they started the third side, the patch began to gap open, and peering through it Agnes could see the edge of the window. There it was already night, with lights going on and cars humming in the street, and people laughing in bars and girls polishing their smiles against the evening's prospects—that was all that Agnes wanted. To be free out there.

We're going to make it, he told himself firmly, and he refused to think about going under, broke and hunted in a strange city.

Pesco tried sawing. It was much easier now with the blade cut spread open—it was possible to bear down on the blade. The filings spurted and they could see the cut move along. They ran back and forth to look.

Agnes grabbed Doug. "Look, you done more than your share of this, so you better make the ropes. Take our blankets and cut them into strips. There's a razor blade under my mattress. Cut the blankets into about three strips each. Yours, mine and Billy's. And if that ain't enough, you come and get me, we'll get some more. OK?"

Doug half-ran towards the cell, slowing when he found someone watching him with frightened curiosity. Carl was in his bunk, but Doug didn't pay any attention to him. He didn't have time for him.

But Carl sat up. "What the hell are you brats up to?"

Doug didn't answer. He looked for the razor blade. "Don't

you know you'll bring heat? You'll make this tank hard to live in. Listen to me!"

He found the razor blade and stripped Billy's blankets off. "You tell Agnes. He's down there."

"I'm not talking to Agnes. I'm talking to you. What do you want to get into a crazy stunt like this for? Don't you know you'll get caught?"

"We're almost out," Doug boasted.

"Out? You think that's all there is to it? You kids make me sick. You'll be caught before morning."

Doug didn't listen. He had a job to do for Agnes, and he hacked at the heavy cloth, ignoring Carl.

Carl stood up and came close to him. "Look, Doug, you're not like those brainless bastards. You could get out of this hole and stay out. Don't go. Whatever you did, they won't be too hard on you your first time. But if you're mixed up in this, they'll pour it to you. I'm trying to tell you for your own good."

Doug looked at Carl, flushed with the sense of being someone at last. "I don't need you to tell me anything. I don't need you."

Carl stepped back, his heavy red face tired and sagging. "OK. Tell me that when you're back here. When you need a friend."

Carl sat on the edge of his bunk and began to take his boots off.

Doug knotted the blanket strips into a rope and carried it out to Agnes. They paid it out of one coil into another, trying to estimate the length. Agnes kept asking him, "You think it's long enough?"

Doug said, "If it's not we can drop."

"Yeah? We don't want to break a leg or something—"

Billy shouted, and they gathered around to watch him prying with the mop handle, the metal yielding little by little. Suddenly the brittle weld parted and the patch came loose, thudding on the concrete floor. The hole was open.

They just stared at it. They hadn't really believed in it till now. Then Pesco stooped down to look through and Agnes jolted into action.

"Hold it! Wait just a minute. Pesco—get Armando." When they came running back, Agnes gave his orders. "I'm going first."

He looked at them. No one said anything.

"All right, you two." He pointed at Billy and Doug. "Right after me, as soon as I signal. Armando, you watch as long as you can, and make sure no one goes running to holler for the bulls. Remember, take it easy. Get down the rope as fast as you can. And keep quiet!"

Agnes scooped the rope up and shoved it through the hole. He wiggled after it. Doug watched his feet disappear, then he heard a faint sounds. Pipes tinkling, and the soft boom of the metal wall. A moment later, a long wrenching sound. The window, Doug thought, he's got it open.

The wall rang sharply, and he heard a muffled, "Come on." Doug glanced at Billy, expecting him to go, but Billy was staring at the hole, his mouth open, breathing heavily. The last of Doug's fears had left him sometime during the sawing, and now without thinking at all he began to squirm through the hole. The ragged edge tore at him, but in his excitement he hardly noticed, any more than he noticed the tunnel. All he saw was the blanket rope leading out the window, still jerking with Agnes's weight.

When the rope went loose, he bellied over the window and wrapped his legs around it. His legs, hanging out, tingled with a sense of height.

He pushed free—spinning, slipping down, spinning, bumping against the rough cement face of the building. The lights of the town spun by and he saw a car moving along three blocks away, then he was staring at the building again. Looking up, he saw a pale face in the window.

They had him before he let go of the rope. It was completely unexpected and yet it didn't surprise him. He caught sight of

Agnes. Two deputies were bending his arms back trying to cuff him, and he was fighting them. Doug felt his own arms being pulled back and he struggled.

Agnes pulled his head free and shouted, "Look out!" And when the deputy tried to cover his mouth, Agnes bit him. The deputy screamed and grabbed his hand. Agnes hit the other one in the solar plexus and broke free.

Instinctively Doug threw his own weight against his captors and caught them as they hesitated, looking after Agnes. He came loose, stumbling and rolling to the side, and ran off after the pale blur of Agnes's shirt jerking through the bushes ahead of him. It was dark and the bushes were thick.

Angry yelling pressed Doug's back. He heard the *slam! slam!* of revolvers, and lights clawed furiously around him, frightening him more than the shooting. The bullets weren't real. He was too young to believe in bullets.

Then he was in some larger bushes and the branches were slapping against him. He bulled through them, still following Agnes. He heard the sharp crack of branches behind him, and then a siren funneled through the little noises, and a big light began to whip eagerly to the side of him.

Then he was on a stretch of grass with a dark fountain in the center of it, and Agnes was disappearing ahead into another patch of bushes. He plunged after him. Then Agnes had him by the wrist and was pulling him off in a different direction, almost doubling back on themselves. They crossed a street on the soft asphalt, and ran long the shadowed side of a house into the damp protection of someone's wash.

Agnes stopped. Doug knew he should be trying to listen, but he could only hear the disorganized chatter of his own thoughts, and the straining of his breath.

Doug grabbed Agnes and shook him soundlessly in clumsy triumph, and he saw the split of Agnes's wide grin, then Agnes turned and vaulted a fence.

They worked far into a quiet neighborhood, sneaking through back yards, before they felt it was safe to collapse in a vacant lot, hiding in one of the burrows dug by little boys.

Agnes was panting. Doug rolled over on his back and looked up at the sky. He heard Agnes's voice shivering with tension.

"We made it, buddy."

PART TWO

CHAPTER ONE

When they were breathing normally again, and the heat of their exertion drained, they realized it was cold. Doug had brought his heavy jacket, but Agnes had jumped off in only a T-shirt, and shortly he was shivering in a different way. The ground they were curled against was hard and damp.

Agnes sat up, hugging his bare arms. "This ain't going to make it, buddy. I'm colder'n a frozen owl."

Doug sat up too, and together they looked around, ready to drop back into their burrow at the slightest hint of motion. The ragged weeds around them were enlarged by the night into a kind of brooding strangeness; an old newspaper was lit with a submerged gleam. The houses they saw seemed like abstract squares cutting their solid shapes against the dimmer hills that rose behind them. Lights were scattered on the hills, but they were cheerless.

"This anywhere near where you got the money hid?"

Agnes sounded subdued, and Doug knew that Agnes liked to be able to say what to do next, always to produce a solution as if it were easy. Now Agnes was turning to him and it made him miserable to have to say, "Not in the dark. I don't even know where we are."

"You and me both, buddy. I wonder if they caught old Billy?"

"What were they doing out there?" Doug asked.

"Waiting on us. They do that sometimes, let you walk right into a trap. One thing's a cinch, someone split on us. I hope Billy gets a crack at him. It's going to seem funny going home without Billy."

It occurred to Doug that with Billy gone Agnes probably wouldn't go home, and that brought a wave of gladness he was ashamed of but couldn't stop.

Headlights reflected on the street across from them, and they dropped with their faces hidden in their arms. Agnes peered over his forearm to see a searchlight drag across the buggy-whip aerial like a lifted tail.

"Old salmon-sides," he muttered.

"What're they doing?"

"Just sniffing around."

Doug watched the car, fascinated. He waited for it to stop, sure they were caught already. But it drifted up the street, the light roving from side to side. Then it seemed funny—like hide-and-seek. They'd gone right by them.

Agnes punched him lightly and smiled. "They couldn't catch cold. Let's get out of here before I freeze to death."

"Where can we go?"

"Damned if I know. Somewhere where it's warm, at least."

They stumbled out of the lot, already a little stiff. Doug found more than his old pleasure in hurrying silently through the strange streets, passing within a few feet of people who would never guess he was near, isolated as they were behind the orange glow of their shades. They ran through yards, jumped hedges, hid behind cars and dashed across the streets. When they were close to the houses they heard the murmur of voices inside, and once the sound of someone practicing the piano. Dogs barked after them.

"You know where I used to sleep before?" Doug volunteered.

"Where?" Agnes was shivering.

"In parked cars. You have to find one that's unlocked."

"Hey! That's a good idea. But what if they catch us in there asleep?"

"We'll find a car lot. The only thing is, we'll have to get up early."

"It's still better than running around all night in the cold."

They moved on, avoiding light. Slipping around one corner, they found themselves in the beginning of a small business center.

"We might find something around here," Agnes said.

"I've got another idea." Doug looked at the stores carefully. "We might be able to get into one of these places."

Agnes was interested. "You think so?"

Doug felt the initiative shift almost as if Agnes had handed him something, and he nodded with more certainty. "Sure."

He moved quickly along the store fronts, shy of the lights, pressing his face briefly against the windows. Agnes tagged after him. They saw a grocery, the shelves leading back to a large refrigerator; a darkened cleaners; and a drugstore are lit up as if it were open.

Agnes liked the drugstore, but Doug told him they were too hard to get into.

"We can't fool around making up our mind." Agnes looked up and down the street. "Those prowl cars are going to be rolling all night."

"Let's look in back. We'll be out of sight."

Certain Agnes would follow him, Doug went over a small fence and along the rough wall of the building. He tripped over a watering can, and behind him Agnes jerked out an alarmed protest, but Doug was feeling fine now. He couldn't worry. He waved his hand behind him, like the commander of an expedition, and looked at the back wall of the cleaners. He dismissed the door without considering it. The windows were barred; the only opening was provided for the fan of an air conditioner. We could go through there, he thought. But that meant a lot of work and noise.

He heard Agnes breathing to the side of him. "I'm going up on top," he told him.

And he did. While Agnes crouched down beside a garbage can, Doug went up a pipe, walking up the wall with some of the stale theatrical zest he'd seen in so many movies. He wondered if Agnes were watching.

He pulled himself over the edge of the roof and, crouching, wiped his hands on his pants. The gravel imbedded in the tarpaper creaked beneath his soft soles as he went lightly on his toes towards a row of skylights, jutting up in their dark triangular housing. In the center of the roof, he turned slowly in a cautious circle: the sky was starless with a high overcast, and the windows around him seemed blind.

Satisfied, he tried to look through the skylights but the glass was pebbled and webbed throughout with small wire octagons. He put his ear to a vent pipe and felt warm damp air flowing over the side of his face, as stale as a fetid breath. He couldn't hear anything.

Twice before he'd stumbled into people sleeping in dark stores, one with a .22 rifle beside his cot. Doug remembered the sudden light gleaming on the oil barrel, the slow-motion fear of his own flight with the angry shouting behind him. But the man hadn't fired.

Now the possibility that someone might be asleep in the store below held him motionless, straining to listen, trying to decide. Then he thought briefly of Agnes—Ernie, Billy called him—waiting below.

He checked the skylights. They were all solid in their frames, but at the bottom of each sash he saw the dim shadow of a catch—on the inside.

Light flowed along the buildings across the street, the wash of headlights, and he crouched down as he heard the motor, the sound rising, slowly passing, dwindling. In the silence that followed, he made up his mind.

He stood up exposed on the roof, aimed deliberately and smashed at the glass with his heel, twice, as hard and as fast as he could kick. Below the sharp splintering he heard a distant tinkle as bits of glass fell on the floor below. But only a little of the glass fell through. Most of it clung to the reinforcing wire, bulging inward, a cracked gray skin with little emptinesses in it.

He ran back to the edge of the roof and down the pipe. He slipped three feet at the time and dropped the last six. Agnes rose, his face shifting out of the shadows, angry and anxious.

"What the hell was that?"

"Come on!"

He grabbed Agnes's arm, pulling him around, across the yard and over a fence to drop beside a small wooden building. Agnes dropped beside him; as they listened they heard a plaintive clucking and ruffling.

Agnes was panting. "Chickens," he said. "What the hell happened?"

"I broke a window."

"What for? I thought you'd gone through the roof. What the—"

"Sssh!"

He held his hand in Agnes's face and turned to look back over the fence. The windows of the cleaners were still dark. Around them the neighborhood slept. Even the chickens were quiet.

He grinned at Agnes. "I broke it so we could get in. If there's anyone in there they'll turn the lights on. And if the lights *don't* go on, we know it's all right. And if the police come...." He pointed up beyond another house where they could see the street. "We can get away out through there."

Agnes punched him, and he grinned into the dark shadows where Agnes's eyes were.

"What do you think's in there?" Agnes asked.

"Money. There'll be money. And you can get clothes. A coat. Any coat you want."

"How long should we wait?"

"I don't know. A while yet."

They settled down to wait, leaning against the fence. Agnes amused himself by pulling up handfuls of grass and throwing them against the side of the chicken coop.

Now that the cleaners had been discussed, Doug didn't know what to say to Agnes. He wanted to go on talking about what he was doing for them, about his skill and boldness, but he couldn't think of any way to start. Agnes seemed as strange to him as someone he might have sat down next to in a bus depot. He realized that he didn't know Agnes, but with Billy gone—

"How long do you think we've been waiting?" Agnes asked.

"I don't know. Not long."

"It seems like an hour."

Doug knew it hadn't been anywhere near that long, but he was anxious to show Agnes more of his daring, and to break the strain between them.

"Let's go. If anybody heard that, they'd be here by now."

Back over the fence, they approached the cleaners warily, a little apart, forgetting each other in their common apprehension. Doug pulled himself up to peer through a window. He saw the vague outline of metal tubs, and an ironing board floated in the dimness like a drowned island.

"It looks OK," he whispered. "You wait here. I'll open the door from the inside."

The crushed skylight was unchanged. He put his eye to one of the broken places and again he felt the warm inside air, but he couldn't see anything helpful. He started to work the pieces of glass out of the wire and whenever one slipped loose and fell, ringing below, he paused for a moment, listening to the night around him.

When he had the catch loose, the window opened about ten inches before it stopped on a restraining chain. He stuck his head in and saw light catching on a narrow metal rafter about three feet down. It was enough.

He took his jacket off and stuck his legs through first, backing in on his belly until he bent at the waist, his legs milling around. He had a strong sense of the distance below him, but he worked himself in until he was teetering on his chest. His ankle struck sharply. Then his feet were secure on the rafter and he slipped inside.

He was about twenty feet up. Too far to drop. He straddled the rafter, looking for some way down. Heavy pipes ran up the wall in several places, but he couldn't reach them. He was isolated on the single girder, which ended blind at both walls. An electrical conduit, flowering in the middle with a green light shade, led across to another girder, but he was afraid to trust his weight on it.

The height began to make him nervous. The three-inch metal surface cut into his thigh and he shifted anxiously. He had to find some way down. He wasn't going back and tell Agnes he couldn't make it.

Then he saw a canvas basket, a gray square on the dark floor, about ten feet away and directly under the rafter. He worked along until he was over it. The basket was full of clothes, and he forced himself to realize that it only seemed small because he was above it.

He didn't hesitate, but dropped to hang at arm's length. He pitched face down in the clothes, and the basket hopped on its metal skids. The clothes were wet and sour, but he stayed quiet for a moment listening to the sounds in the dark plant. Somewhere automatic machinery was humming, but that was a sound that reassured him.

The back door was locked in three different ways, a heavy bar in metal brackets, a sliding bolt and a regular night latch. He undid them and opened a crack of cold air.

"Agnes," he whispered, and a pale shape rose up from behind the garbage can.

Agnes paused inside the door, adjusting to the strangeness of the shop, looking along the racks of clothes flanked by the bulk of equipment. He was still hugging his arms and shivering. Then he went into a silent frenzy, shaking Doug and pounding him on the arms.

"Ain't this something? Buddy, you're too much. Where do you think the money is?"

"Probably up front."

The register was in plain view of the street, but Doug went out on his hands and knees and banged it open. It was empty except for a handful of pennies. He put the pennies in his pocket and slid back along the floor to where he thought Agnes was waiting. But Agnes wasn't there, and it was a moment before he located him by the whirr of coat hangers sliding on a metal rail. Agnes was shopping for some new clothes. Doug moved behind him.

"They must have hid the money."

Agnes was squinting at a pair of pants, trying to see what they looked like in the dark. He threw them aside. "There wasn't nothing?"

"Just some pennies." He rattled them in his pocket. "They must have hid the money. It's somewhere around."

They looked for it. They turned up bundles of old bills— the paper residue of years of business, boxes of paper clips, a discarded dental plate which Agnes smashed under his heel, a box of first-aid supplies, marking pencils, and a stack of old trade journals. They located a small desk and pulled the drawers out and dumped them, lighting matches to paw through the pile. They found nothing of value.

Doug felt bad about it and it was hard for him to stop looking. Even after Agnes had given up in disgust and gone back to sorting through the clothes, Doug went on, looking into such unlikely places as on top of the fuse boxes, under the big washer and in the flush tank of the toilet.

Agnes called to him: "Why don't you give up? There ain't nothing in here."

He said, "I'm sorry."

"What the hell for? You didn't promise me anything, did you?"

They stole new outfits off the racks and changed clothes, rolling their old ones into bundles. "They won't expect us to be dressed like this," Agnes remarked, and it made sense. The cleaners had been of some use.

Then when he was digging out some bundles, looking for a shirt, he found the canvas sack.

They didn't open it until they were settled down for the night in a small panel truck they found parked outside a laundry. Twice, in the dark blocks between the cleaners and the laundry, they'd seen police cars in the street. Once it was turning a corner above them. The other time they crouched behind a car and watched the police drive slowly by.

When they got the sack open, it was almost too dark to read the bills. They had a little over twenty dollars. "Well, that's get-around money," Agnes said.

They rolled the window up and tried to sleep in the back of the truck, but it was cold and hard. Agnes sat up, complaining. "This is something. It's even harder than the bunks in jail."

"We could try something else," Doug suggested. "Maybe break into another place."

"Not tonight. This town's crawling with heat. I've got an idea."

Agnes ripped the ignition wires from under the dashboard, and after experimenting with the different pairs, he found the right two and got the motor going. He turned on the heater.

"This probably ain't too smart, but I'm too cold to care."

"It doesn't make much noise. How'd you learn to do that?"

"Billy. He can start a car that way just as easy as with a key."

"Why couldn't we just take off in this and drive right out of town?"

"You kidding? I already got busted once just like that. Right here in this town. They block the roads. We went around a corner and there they were. We tried to turn around and they were behind us too. And, buddy, that was it."

"What're we going to do then?"

"Take it easy. Hide out for a couple of days. They won't sit out there forever. We got eating money so we don't have to worry."

They fell silent and a few minutes later Agnes was asleep. Doug heard him snoring softly and as he listened he felt lonelier even than he did by himself. Agnes was a stranger asleep.

The inside of the truck was warm now, so he climbed into the front seat, unhooking the wires and killing the motor. He sat for awhile playing with the gear shift, looking out the window. Two dogs ran across the street, one after the other. Everything around him was silent and dark.

He was thinking back to the cleaners when he remembered his jacket. It was still on the roof.

CHAPTER TWO

When they left the truck in the morning it was still gray, and Agnes was half-awake, sullen and grouchy. His new clothes were garish—confused by the dim light in the cleaners, he'd grabbed an orange shirt, light-blue pants and a greenish coat. Doug started laughing.

"What's funny?" Agnes demanded.

"Your clothes."

"What's the matter with them?"

"Nothing. Except they don't match."

"They're all right." Agnes circled around, smoothing the stolen coat; he checked himself to see how it hung in back. Then he looked Doug over.

"You don't look like no dude yourself."

Doug had picked a suit styled for a man years older. He liked it because he thought it made him look grown up. He straightened his shoulders and looked down at himself; except for the white shoes he looked pretty good.

They were heading towards the edge of town, looking for some shelter where they could spend the day, when they saw a figure run across the street in front of them. It was instantly familiar.

"Billy—*Billy!*" Agnes shouted.

Billy turned, hesitated almost comically, and then raced towards them.

"Ernie—I've been looking for you all night!"

Agnes grabbed him by the arm and feinted once at his stomach. "I'd given you up, buddy. I thought they had you."

Billy's face could hardly hold his grin and his relief. He bobbed his big-eared head and marveled at Agnes. "Boy, ain't you something. Where'd you get them clothes?"

"We busted into a cleaners."

"Yeah? Did you get any loot?"

"About twenty stones. Come on. We've got to find some

place to hide before this town starts jumping."

Doug had stood apart while Agnes and Billy greeted each other. Odd wheel. Well, he was used to it, wasn't he? But he didn't like it, and he wished they hadn't run into Billy. He wouldn't want Billy caught, but why couldn't he have just— gone off by himself?

They found a hiding place behind a pile of broken and rusting automobiles stacked in the back of a wrecking lot. They were hidden from the street and from the lot itself; in front of them a field of scattered dry grass lowered into a flat-bottomed gully, where the railroad tracks went in a long curve over their dark-gray ties.

"How'd you get away?" Agnes asked Billy.

"They didn't even see me. They were all too busy trying to pot you guys. I jumped off into the bushes and went under like a goddam rabbit. As soon as I could, I lit out after you guys. I was looking for you all night. And let me tell you something. This town is alive with cops—"

"They'll be slacking off after while. They get tired, too. I was thinking—if we could find a show, we could hide out there until late tonight."

"That's cool," Billy agreed.

Agnes turned to Doug. "You figure out where you got that money hid?"

Doug wasn't ready for the question; he'd avoided thinking about his imaginary cache, and he floundered a moment before he could begin to frame an answer.

"I don't know. I'm not sure, but I think it's on the other side of town. I'd have to be downtown to tell for sure, but I think it's on the other side."

His voice sounded lame and unconvincing even to himself, and he felt he was losing all the ground he'd won in the night.

Agnes said, "This town ain't that big."

But Billy picked up Doug's argument for him. "We can forget that for now. This is no time for a stroll downtown."

"Do you think Armando got away?" Agnes asked.

"I don't know. I think Pesco did. He was right on top of me."

"If Armando didn't make it, he'll be hot enough to kill. He's liable to catch that bastard with the necktie, and cut his head off."

"You think that guy ratted?" Billy asked.

"Someone did."

"Yeah. But I'd bet on Slim."

"Slim?" Agnes questioned and then fell silent, thinking about it.

Doug was hungry, but he didn't mention it, because there didn't seem to be anything to do about it. The money he'd found seemed useless if they couldn't get out to spend it— and he felt useless himself now that Billy was back. They talked around him, and he couldn't think of anything to say.

What's the matter with me? he wondered.

A little after noon, they slipped back towards the center of town, and a few blocks from where they'd spent the morning they found a small neighborhood theatre. Doug went for the tickets while Billy and Agnes hung back pretending to be interested in the marquee display.

The girl in the booth looked to be about his own age, and he put a special emphasis on his, "Three, please." His eyes were on her soft mouth.

"Students or adults?" she asked. Her voice was high, still unformed.

"Adults," he said, feeling grown up. Her eyes met his when she took his money. Three purple tickets spat out of the machine and his change rolled into the little cup.

"Thanks," he murmured, wishing there was something more he could say, some way to hold her attention. She looked down, her face bland.

A tall kid in a badly fitting uniform tore their tickets, and they hurried into a shabby lobby. On either side of a florid mural depicting some Indian rite there was a machine, one coke and the other popcorn. They kept both of them going until they had as much as they could carry.

The theatre was almost empty. They sat far down to the front, and didn't pay much attention to the picture until the popcorn was gone. Doug felt himself relaxing. He'd always liked movies. He slipped down in his seat and put his knees up on the back of the one in front of him. The salt from the popcorn made the coke taste delicious.

The picture was a horror movie about a man who changed into a beast at twelve o'clock on nights of the full moon, unless he rubbed on his wrist the juice of a very rare plant. He didn't want to be a beast, and so he raised the plants that would save him in a secret greenhouse, but by the end his supply of plants had been destroyed, and he was frantically trying to get into the Royal Zoological Garden where he hoped to find a single specimen. The scene shifted from the moonrise, to the clock, and then back to the man... He is shaking the gate, calling out to the caretaker, and then he sees his hands gnarling, the nails sprouting like wild roots, the dark hair springing up in a series of jerks.... He goes humping off into the night, turning every now and then to snarl into the camera, his beast face a secret mask of anguish.... He killed the girl and in the end they shot him off a building, his arms flailing and his cloak raveling behind him like a defective parachute. Then there was a quiet scene, where they grouped around him, watching while his upturned face changed slowly back, until he was just an ordinary man lying dead.

During the newsreel Doug went out and bought more coke and popcorn. They felt perfectly safe now—the movie had carried them away. Agnes draped his legs over the seat in front of his and started shouting jokes at the screen. They laughed at everything he said. Agnes was better than the show.

The second feature was a western, and during it the theatre began to fill up. Doug became aware of girls' voices. They were in the row directly behind them, two of them, their faces faintly purple in the semidarkness. He saw the smooth blank circles of their knees angled up at him, and turned back to the screen, no longer interested in what was on it.

The girls began to giggle at Agnes, and he doubled his remarks, seizing on every turn of the plot to shout some hoarse western burlesque.

"What a smart alec," one of them said tartly.

"No, ma'am," Agnes replied without hesitation. "I'm Ernie. I don't know any Alec." He turned to Billy and asked with elaborate concern, "This here young lady's looking for Alec. You know him?"

"Can't say that I do."

"How about you, Doug?" Agnes persisted with his joke.

"Doesn't he think he's smart, though?"

"I'm so bright my mother used to call me Son."

"Well, I could think of something to call you and it wouldn't be Son."

"No, ma'am, I sure wouldn't want you calling me Son—how about Daddy?"

The girls laughed and the movie was forgotten. Agnes turned around in his seat, trying to size them up in the dim light. "What's your names?" he asked in his normal voice.

The tart one answered, "I'm Donna and this is Jeanie."

"And this is my old buddy, Billy. And that's Doug. Fellows, meet the new school marm and her lady companion. You live around here?"

"Maybe."

Donna did the talking. Jeanie giggled softly and pushed at her hair. Jeanie seemed to be round and plump while Donna was thinner, but there wasn't any way to tell what they really looked like, or even how old they were.

Doug went for cokes, and when he returned, cautiously balancing the paper cups, he found the four of them in the same row. The girls were in the middle and Agnes and Billy were on either side of them, with Billy sitting next to Jeanie.

He knew it would turn out like this and so he was almost relieved to have it settled, but if Billy hadn't been there—well, then it might have been different.

He sat down next to Agnes and passed the cokes along. He tried to interest himself in the movie, but under the artificial talk from the screen he heard the low voices of Agnes and Donna. Her tartness had turned to banter.

"Do you go to school?" Agnes asked.

"I'm not there, am I?"

"That don't mean you're not supposed to be."

"You're sure nosy."

Agnes leaned closer and whispered something to her, something that ended in "horny" and she threw her head back against the seat laughing.

"Oh, Ernie. You shouldn't talk like that."

"Why not? It's true."

"Even so, you just shouldn't. You make me sound like a cow or something."

"Well, I wasn't too particular about talking anyway." He leaned over her and whispered again. Her eyes rounded.

"Shoot! How you come on!" she exclaimed, her voice full of pleased disapproval. She slid down in the seat, still looking up, and Agnes kissed her.

Doug watched, his eyes cut to the side, tense with interest. He imagined himself in Agnes's place.

"Mmmm," Donna sighed theatrically. "You're pretty swell."

They twisted together, melting around the awkwardness of the seat arm, and to Doug a kind of odor seemed to rise from them, dark and hot. They made a circle of it, and he smelled it with his stomach. It crawled along his legs and his face felt swollen with it.

Donna had slipped down on the small of her back, and Agnes was over her. Doug saw his hand moving on her skirt, and then her pale thigh, gleaming dimly.

"Ernie—not here."

Then her light quick breathing and the wet noise of their mouths.

"Ernie, you shouldn't—Ernie. Boy, you do know how to make out."

Agnes was silent. His heavy back looked almost grim to
Doug, and the girl's face was shadowed under his shoulder,
her mouth a round blur.

An arm reached over in front of him. He caught a heart-
freezing flash of gold braid before he saw the face of the young
usher. The usher tapped Agnes.

"You'd better cool it."

Agnes whirled on him. "What the hell do you want?"

The usher took a half step back. "Don't jump salty with
me. Some people complained to the manager. You better cool
it—he'll call the cops."

Agnes's face went empty. "Yeah?"

"Look, man, take a tip. I know these two brats. If either one
of 'em's sixteen, I'm a hundred and five."

"Sixteen!" Agnes laughed. "Why, that's an old lady where
I come from."

"Well, out here we call them jailbait. You understand?"

"Don't pay any attention to him, Ernie." Donna's voice was
angry with a thread of hurt in it. "He's just jealous."

"Jealous!" The usher was amused. "Would I be jealous of
the town pump?" Then he leaned over Agnes and said in a
quiet, man-to-man voice, "Take them somewhere after the
show, but cool it in here, huh? It ain't me, it's the manager."

"Okay," Agnes said.

Donna was straightening her skirt, looking away. "Let's get
out of here," she said, "I can't stand that creep."

The usher shrugged and started up the aisle. Agnes said
uncomfortably, "We might as well see the picture. We paid
for it."

Doug smiled to himself. It shouldn't have seemed funny
but it did. They couldn't leave. And even if they could they
didn't have anyplace to take them. He looked over to see what
Donna was doing. She was combing her hair, and Agnes was
scowling at the screen.

After the western, Donna said, "Let's get out of here."

Agnes answered sullenly, "We didn't get to see the first part of this other one."

"I'm beginning to think you'd rather stay here and watch this old show—" Donna left her alternative hanging in the air, and it was unmistakable. Doug could hear Jeanie giggling with embarrassment.

"I came to see the show, not roll with some little chippie. If you don't feel like waiting, cut out."

Donna stood up grabbing her coat. "Come on, Jeanie." They started working their way out in a frosty silence, and Agnes stared after them woodenly.

They sat through both of the features again without saying much to each other. Agnes was either lost in the picture or still smarting from the awkward ending with the girls.

CHAPTER THREE

It was full night when they left the theatre. The clock in the ticket booth read nine-thirty.

"Where to?" Billy asked.

"Out of here," Agnes replied. "And fast."

They passed a fountain full of high school kids jammed along the length of the counter: the white, red, and cream of the girls' sweaters among the leather jackets of the boys. Doug wondered if Donna and Jeanie were in there. The light and the laughter seemed so warm and secure. He realized that those kids were around his own age, and the contrast between his life and theirs seemed sharp and painful. He looked down at the folds of his stolen suit where it hung on him down to his scuffed white shoes. He felt silly.

Agnes set the pace, ducking along behind the parked cars, going in the same direction they'd been on when they discovered the movie.

Once Doug looked back, just before they turned a corner, and the fountain and the movie theatre made an island of light.

Agnes paused and asked Doug, "What do you think we ought to look for?"

"What for?"

"To break into. What should we look for?"

"It's pretty early. Maybe we ought to wait a couple more hours."

"We can look around. Find something. What do you think?"

Doug didn't have any ideas. He hardly knew the town, but he was confident something would turn up. "Let's just look around. We'll hit something."

"Let's not shoot any more blanks," Agnes said. "Twenty dollars ain't much."

Twenty dollars was as much as he'd ever found, but no, he'd built it into a fortune, and now what was he going to do? He was disgusted with himself. Somehow he'd have to lead them to some real money.

They kept to the shadows, strung out one behind the other, and Doug noticed that he was bringing up the rear again. Whenever headlights came in the street they ran back among the houses to hide.

Gradually the houses and businesses gave way to heavier buildings: machine shops, garages, small factories and warehouses. It was an area already empty of people, and they felt it safe to walk on the sidewalk. A block over they saw the lights of a truck route, but their own street was free of traffic.

Several of the warehouses were open on all four sides and they looked easy to approach, but something about them didn't seem right to Doug. He kept waiting for his psychic pointer to flicker and say *there*. But the buildings were too big, and he knew there would be a strong possibility of a night watchman.

Agnes was impatient, so Doug didn't say anything when Agnes started to circle one of the warehouses, moving from hiding place to hiding place, looking it over.

It was an L-shaped building, lined on the outside of the L with a long loading platform, matched by a solid wall of corrugated sliding doors. A gravel apron stretched out towards the truck route. A small bulb burned high on the building, throwing a cone of light over the legend: WHOLESALE GROCERY DIST. painted in large black capitals. The loading platform was a sheet of gray ice, barren and exposed. Four feet below it was a darkness filled with a litter of broken cardboard boxes. They crawled along there, conscious of the busy truck route half a block away.

They found the back of the building protected by a tall wire fence. Pressed against it, they could see faint smudges of light reflected from dark windows, stumbling piles of wooden crates, and what looked like the door of a giant refrigerator.

"What do you think?" Agnes whispered. "Huh? How do you like it?"

"It looks good," Billy answered. "If we can get in."

"How about it? Can we get in, Doug?"

The flattery hadn't thinned. He was afraid of the building, but he looked it over, trying to form a plan. Vanity helped make his answer: "There's always some way in." But then caution caused him to add, "It's pretty early."

"That's good. If we don't score here, we'll have time for something else."

Doug turned back to the building. Some clouds had moved away from the moon and he could see a little more—a narrow shed, the metal roof like a ribbon of silver—but the windows were barred and screened as well.

"OK," he agreed. "I'll take a look."

"We'll wait here," Agnes said. His voice was pleased. Doug turned and saw the moonlight on his long hair, his profile dark against the wire diamonds of the fence, and Billy's face, by a freak of light, lit up beside him. Doug felt something swelling inside himself. They were the first real friends he'd ever had.

He took his shoes off, tied the laces together, and hung them around his neck. He started up the fence, his toes digging into the wire holes. Agnes clapped him on the back and told Billy,

"Just like Tarzan."

Doug was still smiling when he dropped down the other side. He banged the fence in salute, and started off through a maze of discarded vegetable counters. The area he was in was described on two sides by the wire fence, and the L of the warehouse completed a rectangle. He hurried across a square of moon-bleached gravel, and in the shadow of the building he stopped to put his shoes on.

The back of the warehouse was tight. He fumbled with the massive lock on the door of the refrigerator and left it as hopeless. The door into the main part of the building had a lot of empty cans and boxes stacked around it. Doug pushed against the door, testing it, but it was solid. The shed was separated from the warehouse by a foot of empty darkness, and there didn't seem to be any easy way to gain the roof. He crouched away from the building, looking it over, trying to improvise some way up.

In one of the windows he caught the hint of a light. At first he thought it was reflected from the street far behind him, but he turned quickly to find the street empty. Then the window was dark too, leaving him uncertain that he'd really seen anything. He knew that sometimes his eyes played tricks in the dark.

He moved quickly to the window and hoisted himself on the bars, pressing his face against the webbed protection screen. He saw a brief moving flicker, like a distant firefly—and then it was gone. He couldn't form any idea as to what might have caused it, but it was enough to make him decide against the warehouse. He hurried back toward the fence.

Agnes and Billy were gone. Without thinking he rushed up and down the fence, calling softly. He stopped, staring into the empty lot.

For a moment he was empty. Then misery rushed in, and it felt as though the temperature had suddenly dropped. In an instant's montage of impressions he saw his future: alone—always isolated.

He was shocked, yet even in his shock was the beginning of acceptance, an acceptance that had been building like invisible armor ever since they'd found Billy that morning.

He scaled the fence and started back around it. He wanted to get away from the warehouse and he was content with the money he had. He didn't need much money. All he could think of was to find another show where he could kill most of the night

A sudden wrenching noise pulled him. Ahead something moved in the shadows and he heard a tense whisper.

"Jesus, Billy! Take it easy."

He rushed up to see the quick flash of Agnes's face coming towards him.

"Doug! Damn, buddy, I almost dropped you."

"Sorry. I was glad to find you."

"Oh, yeah—well, Billy got restless. We thought we'd hunt this side. What'd you find?"

"Nothing. This place is solid."

He heard Billy's voice below him. "No, it ain't. We got a little door right here. Soon as I get it ripped off."

He squatted down beside Billy, and found him prying up a grate that vented the lower part of the warehouse. He shook his head, forgetting that Billy couldn't see him clearly.

"That won't lead anywhere. Just all along under the floor."

"How do you know?" Agnes asked. "There might be a trap door through the floor."

"Or a sub-basement," Billy added.

He started to tell them about the light, but he was afraid they'd think him chicken. Then a colder thought struck him. He swallowed nervously and asked, "Who's going in?"

"I will," Billy answered matter-of-factly. He was prying with an old stick and again the grate wrenched. "One more and I've got it."

"Heave hard and get it over with," Agnes advised. "If you keep that racket up we'll have every cop in town looking over our shoulder."

Billy set his lever and threw his weight on it. The grate popped out with surprisingly little noise.

Agnes laughed. "You sweet-talked it out, Billy."

Doug caught the flash of Billy's teeth, and smiled himself. Billy lit a match and held it in the opening, and they leaned in around him to look. The feeble light died a few feet inside, exposing only packed earth and some raw-wood foundations.

"I wish I had a flashlight," Billy said with an undertone of anxiety.

"You can make it." Agnes punched him lightly, encouraging him.

"OK, I'll take a look."

Three feet in he was out of sight. They watched the matches blooming irregularly, gaining distance, the light streaking back along the dust-furred wiring. Then they strained against the darkness and couldn't see anything.

"He must have turned a corner or something," Agnes remarked, settling back on his heels. He took a cigarette out of his pocket and lit up.

Doug nodded numbly. He shouldn't have let Billy go in there. Agnes had just forced him to realize what he'd seen through the window. The flare of a match as someone lit a cigarette. Had he known that's what it was, and still not said anything? I couldn't have stopped him, he told himself.

He looked around. Uneasy now. The night seemed raw with menace. To the rear they were sheltered by the small leg of the warehouse, but to the side, Doug could see the gravel apron leading to the street. The traffic was still heavy, seeming to come in groups of two or three cars and then the single trucks, slow with power. The warehouse hid them from the moon, and he should have felt secure, but he didn't.

"What do you think he's doing in there?" Agnes asked in a subdued voice.

Doug shifted. He was growing cramped. "I don't know," he mumbled.

They fell silent again, because they knew one of them should volunteer to go in and look. Doug turned away. He wasn't going. Agnes didn't move.

Suddenly it all split open. Light washed them, and they swiveled like twin marionettes to see headlights bearing down. As they were on the point of running, the headlights veered away, round in a sweeping bend, leading the now almost familiar white-sided car with its telltale double antenna. The prowl car skidded, spraying gravel, slowing as it went out of sight around the front of the warehouse. They heard the motor cut off; the doors slammed one right after the other.

Agnes moved out. Doug followed him as he slipped along the side of the building, clearing the corner in time to see the two cops vault onto the loading platform and run through one of the large doors. It had been standing open for them.

The whole story was there. Doug read it as if he knew it by heart. Billy had made it in, but there had been a watchman.

"Let's get out of here," Agnes urged, pulling at his arm.

They ran as fast as they could for six hard blocks, forgetting caution in their blind retreat. The police were suddenly part of reality again—for a whole day they had been able to forget them, or remember them only as an abstraction, but now they were after them again. Maybe only a few blocks away. Racing in their cars while they ran helplessly on foot. The radio projecting their giant voices

Finally Agnes ducked into the shadow of a private garage, flattening his back against the wooden wall. He was panting heavily. When he could speak, he said, "We couldn't have done nothing for Billy."

Doug tried to be silent—it was the last thing he could do. Agnes was looking at him with a strange naked look, and he found himself nodding.

"No, there was nothing we could do."

CHAPTER FOUR

They hid for hours in the back of a grocery store, in a little shed full of the smell of rotting lettuce. Doug tried to talk, but Agnes was lost in a sullen silence. Doug sensed that Agnes was frightened and it killed his spirit like a whip.

He began to get sleepy and that made him even more miserable. He just wanted to lie down and go to sleep; he didn't care where just as long as it was in out of the cold. He watched Agnes wrapping and unwrapping a piece of rope around his hand. He made a corded fist, and hit the wooden garbage bin he was sitting next to, hit it hard, unwound the rope, rewound it and hit the bin again. His face was sunk in his upturned coat collar and Doug didn't feel that he knew him.

Doug sat silently, prepared to endure. The smell of the lettuce came and went in his nostrils, and he tried to find some amusement in turning the patterns of the shadows into fanciful shapes. But he was too tired to enjoy it. His back began to ache. He tried to reach Agnes again.

"This is worse than jail."

Agnes turned his head, but he didn't say anything. "Let's find a car we can sleep in."

Agnes stood up and threw the rope at his feet. "The hell with that. I'm tired of crawling around this town like a sick dog. Hiding in this garbage heap like some punk." He indicated the shed with a violent motion of his hand. "Let's get the hell out of here."

Agnes started off, kicking a box out of his way, and Doug automatically rose to follow. He was glad to be moving.

They found themselves in a cheap-rent district on the edge of the small industrial complex they'd been forced out of.

Across the street they saw a sign cut in the shape of a beer mug. With NED'S painted across it. Agnes stopped.

"That's what I need." He started across the street and Doug had to hurry to catch up.

It was an old-style bar built into the hollowed-out shell of some abandoned store. The large, clear-glass windows were edged with faded crepe paper, and in the center of each window, the name of a beer written in red-glass tubing flickered sluggishly. A long bar was visible, empty through most of the center, but with a small cluster of people at each end.

Agnes walked in, almost strutting, meeting the faces that turned to him. Doug noticed the faded linoleum floor, criss-crossed with bullet shaped burns and smashed cigarette butts. He followed Agnes, climbing onto one of the empty stools in the center of the bar. He carefully avoided looking either way. He knew he didn't belong in the place.

A thin man in a dark-green shirt moved up behind the bar. "Hiya, folks." He gave Agnes a tired mechanical smile; then he saw Doug and his face soured.

"Your buddy's kinda young."

"He's old enough," Agnes replied.

"He don't look it."

"Well, he is." Agnes was inviting the bartender to call him a liar. "OK? Couple of beers."

The bartender had a pale, drifter's face and anxious, brittle eyes. He hung for a moment, uncertain. Then he shrugged and asked, "Bottle or draft?"

"Draft."

The bartender moved off, and a heavy blonde woman called him over and told him something, gesturing up at them with her head. Doug was sure she was indicating him and he looked down, feeling more like a fake than ever. To him the bar was dismal, but Agnes shifted around on his stool, grinning freely again.

"This is more like it."

"Do you think it's safe?"

"What's the sense in being safe if we can't do nothing? We might as well have stayed in jail. Being safe didn't help Billy none."

Doug shut up. He didn't want to think about Billy. He

watched the people down at his end of the bar. Two women, girls maybe, he didn't have any idea how old they were, and a man. The girls were sitting up to the bar and the man was standing between them, swaying from one to the other, telling them something. He broke off to laugh, and staggered back, clutching their shoulders for balance. A short round man in a faded green windbreaker, with a loose mouth that he couldn't seem to keep closed. The girls were nice, dressed fancy, turning their drinks in their white hands. One of them had long blonde hair, neatly rolled, and the other girl was darker; her hair was cut short and combed over her forehead.

The bartender clumped a glass in front of him. "Listen. This kid looks too young. Why don't you just drink these and leave?"

Agnes shoved a dollar across the bar. "I said he was old enough. You can let it go like that and just maybe have some trouble, or you can push it and have some for sure. Take your choice. I don't much care how you jump."

The bartender snatched the dollar and turned away. He made change and dumped it in front of them; then he went to stand in front of the large blonde woman, his eyes darting uneasily between her and Agnes. The woman looked down the bar. Her eyes were so small they didn't reflect any light.

Agnes ignored them. He took a big gulp of beer and brushed his mouth with the back of his hand. "Tastes just like it used to."

Beer was as much as Doug had ever had to drink. He neither liked nor disliked it. He sipped slowly, watching the two girls at the end of the bar. He liked the light-haired one, liked the way she smiled.

"What a bunch of deadheads." Agnes was looking around, restless again. He carried his glass over to an old jukebox and studied the selections. Pumping in a coin, he started a hillbilly tune going and came back in a shuffling dance step, spinning with his glass held out like a partner's hand.

"That's better." Agnes drained his beer and rapped the glass on the bar. The bartender moved sullenly, filling the glass and taking some of their change.

The short man tried to dance with the light-haired girl, but he was too drunk—he could only hang on her and shuffle around. The girl's face was above the back of his head, and when she turned towards Doug her look of boredom was relieved by a small smile. Automatically Doug looked behind himself, and found Agnes grinning at the girl. His own face felt frozen.

Agnes leaned over and whispered, "Look at him. He's got two of them and I bet he can't even use one."

Doug turned back with sharper interest. The girl on the floor wore a tight black dress, and the edges of the short sleeves creased her full arms; the waist was tight and the skirt flared. Her face and hair were fixed to make her look like a different kind of girl than she really was, but even so Doug thought her face was warm and nice, not sharp or critical, even of the man who was hanging onto her, pretending to dance.

The record ended and she released herself. Then the jukebox clicked and the new record rode up in its tray. A slow waltz started.

Agnes was beside them, settling his shoulders in his green coat, running his fingers through his hair.

"It was my quarter," he announced. "I should get one dance."

The man started to complain, but Agnes had already swung her away. Neatly circling around and around, he led her into a little dip and glide. She smiled, liking it, spinning out of Agnes's arm, her skirt filling.

Doug didn't trust his dancing, so he avoided looking at the other girl. He drank a little more beer and listened to the short man trying to get her to dance. She shook her head, and adjusted her blouse, watching Agnes and her friend.

"No—dammit, Arnie. I said no, and that's what I meant."

Agnes's feet scuffed on the floor, marking the persistent beat of the record. Doug looked at his fingernails; they were broken off and dirty. The short man started calling for another drink. Grabbing for his glass and missing, he hit it with his arm and sent it rattling down the bar. The bartender, moving quickly, scooped it up before it rolled off.

"You've had enough, Arnie."

"Don't give me that crap. I know when I've had enough…. Had enough, had enough…." He turned it into a whining nasal chant. "You act like this crummy bar was something."

"Yeah? Well I don't want Lucy in here chewing me out because you came home tanked."

"The hell with Lucy—and you too. Give me a drink."

The bartender shook his head. "Look, Arnie, why don't you go on home?"

"I ain't going home. I may never go home. An' you know what? Take your lousy drink and shove it. Come on, Bet, let's go."

He grabbed for the dark girl's arm, but she shrugged away from him. "Lay off, Arnie. I like it here."

He pulled himself up with ponderous drunken dignity, and like the echo of some dated romance he said, "Very well—" Wavering a little. "Very well, you just…." And he faded off, apparently forgetting what he'd started to say. He zipped his windbreaker and started for the door.

Agnes was still dancing, but Doug saw him grinning after the little man, and as if it were part of the same reflex his hand pressed more firmly into the small of the girl's back. She didn't resist, but put her head over Agnes's shoulder, coming up on her toes.

Doug looked down the bar at the dark girl the man had called Bet. She'd been looking at him, but then she turned away to her drink, tapping the glass with bright red fingernails. Her blouse was ruffled in the front and her elbows looked sharp. On the stool rung, her foot moved in time with the music.

Doug waited for the music to stop, wondering what would happen. He was waiting for Agnes to make it easy for him, and at the same time realizing that there were things Agnes couldn't do for him—things that might come later. He looked at his face in the mirror, but he found no confidence in it. His face was pale, and his shirt collar was crumpled. He combed his hair.

Agnes did get them all together, as naturally as if it had been understood all along. He talked to the girls for a few moments and then motioned to Doug. Doug walked towards them, feeling their eyes on him in a way that was almost painful. But then the light-haired girl smiled and said her name was Marion.

"This is Bet."

"Short for Betty," she said. Doug mumbled his own name, and sat down next to Bet, while Agnes called the bartender. He ordered whiskey for them all, but the bartender just turned and looked down the bar to where the heavy blonde was getting up. She came towards them, wearing a coat that was too small for her and flat shoes, a little run-over.

She spoke to Marion, "I don't want this kid drunk in here."

"A little drink won't hurt him," Marion coaxed, looking sideways at Agnes.

"I don't give a damn about him. It's my license I'm worried about."

"He's old enough," Agnes said.

"I don't care how old he is. Can he prove it?"

They all turned to look at Doug. He stumbled a little, and then managed to say, "I lost my wallet."

The heavy woman nodded. "I kinda thought maybe you had."

Agnes stood up. "To hell with this joint. Let's go somewhere else."

Marion looked inquiringly at Bet and she made a gesture that said, Who cares? Doug pretended he was interested in something on the bartop, and he didn't look up until it was obvious that the girls were getting ready to leave. Bet paused to drain her drink.

Outside they stood in a little group for a moment, while Agnes said, "You'll have to call it. We just got here, and we don't know one street from another."

Marion looked at Doug and said, not unkindly, "No one around here is going to serve him. They closed up two places for that very thing. Just a few months ago, too."

"Let's get a bottle then," Agnes suggested.

Bet nodded emphatically, and Marion smiled softly and said, "Why not?"

When they had the liquor, they started down the sidewalk in twos. Doug didn't hide it from himself that Bet wasn't happy with the arrangement, and in a moment she confirmed it by asking him questions about Agnes. He made the answers up, hardly paying any attention to what he said, because he was wondering if he should take her by the arm, as Agnes had taken Marion. He didn't. He walked with his hands in his pockets.

At a corner Marion stopped, swinging away from Anges to look at him. Then she smiled, and turned down another street.

Bet called peevishly, "What about the kids?"

"We'll be quiet," Marion replied.

They turned in at a little house set back from the street. Agnes held a match while Marion looked in her purse.

"Bet, do you have a key?"

"No, but the back door should be open."

They went through the garage. Agnes held up a match, and in its light Doug saw lines of empty bottles standing along the garage wall. It occurred to him that these girls seldom came home alone. He looked at Bet differently. Her face seemed hot and careless. Maybe it would be easier than he thought.

In the kitchen, Bet tossed her coat on a chair, and went directly to a cupboard for some glasses. Marion went through another door, and Agnes followed her, even though she tried to wave him back. Doug was standing where he could see them, and he saw Marion with Agnes behind her, looking into a crib. He heard Agnes ask, "Are they yours?"

"Yes."

"Well…." For the first time Agnes sounded hesitant.

Marion laughed. "Don't worry. He's away. He ships out."

Agnes put his arm around her waist from behind, but she pulled away, going to the other side of the crib.

Doug turned back to Bet. She was already drinking, sitting in a kitchen chair with her legs stretched out in front of her. Her soft skirt fell into the contours of her legs—she was thin, but Doug didn't care. "Get wet, junior," Bet said, indicating the glasses with her head.

He poured as much into his glass as Bet had in hers, and started to drink it as he had the beer. It locked in his throat, but he managed to swallow before he started coughing. He blinked at Bet and she laughed at him.

"How old are you really? Don't lie now."

And for once he didn't. He even managed to smile as he said, "Seventeen."

"You don't even look that old."

"I'm sorry," he said. "I guess this isn't much for you."

Bet looked arch. "What isn't much for me?"

"Oh, you know, getting stuck with me."

Bet smiled more naturally. "I'll survive it. You have nice eyes."

He didn't know how to take the idle compliment, but he didn't have to answer it. Agnes and Marion came out of the bedroom. She was smoothing her dress and Agnes looked cocky. He grinned at Doug and then looked at Bet to see what she thought. Bet sipped her drink and tapped her shoes together, giving Agnes a very quiet look from under her lashes. Marion poured two more glasses.

Doug tried the whiskey again. It didn't hit him quite as hard, but he still winced.

"Why don't you put some water with it?" Agnes offered.

"It's fine." He took another drink, and as he stood waiting for the burning to stop, he felt the liquor banging into his empty stomach. It was beginning to seem great.

Abruptly, he sat down next to Bet. A slow warmth leaked out of his stomach, relaxing him. He felt himself smiling.

Agnes turned a chair around and sat with his feet up on the rungs, like sitting a saddle with short stirrups, he crossed his arms on the back. Doug saw a momentary disapproval shadow Marion's eyes, but Agnes wasn't aware of it. He started making talk.

They all started talking and most of Doug's strangeness wore off. He found himself watching Marion, and she seemed to get softer and softer into a mellow goldenness. Her voice loosened and after awhile she started talking about her husband being gone and what the hell was she supposed to do alone day and night with the kids. There was defense in her voice. Doug read it for what it was, but he couldn't give any real meaning to it. She seemed wonderful to him. He was glad that she was talking and it was necessary just to listen and nod if her light eyes crossed his. She started telling how Bet had moved in, between jobs and needing some place to stay. There was a third girl, Jinx, but she was away.

Bet interrupted to make a sour remark, but Marion went right on, saying Jinx was all right, you just had to understand her, and Bet said she understood her only too well.

"So tell her." Marion leaned over to tap Bet's arm. "She'll be home in a day or two. You can tell her yourself."

Bet shook her head loosely. "It hasn't been that long." A strand of hair trembled on her forehead, and she smoothed it back into place.

"Oh, yes it has," Marion replied with exaggerated positiveness. "Almost four weeks. What'd she have? Thirty days? Figure it out for yourself."

Bet was quiet, her eyes inward, counting. The strand of hair had drifted loose again. "Damn, you know, you're right. She'll be back tomorrow. Marion, you're a fool if you let her go on the way she has been. You better not let her start in again. You'll see, she'll lose you your kids."

Marion was leaning back in her chair, her eyes half-closed.

"I don't think she'll want to. She must have learned some kind of lesson."

"Oh, diddle! Don't give me that." Bet made a clumsy negative gesture with her hand, and tipped the bottle into her glass, the liquor poured in fat rivulets.

"I'm getting curious about this girl," Agnes said.

Marion ignored his implied question. She drank slowly; then said, "She just stays here like Bet. I've got lots of room."

No one said anything for a moment. Bet tapped the edge of her glass against her teeth, watching Agnes out of the corner of her eye. The inside of her lip glistened in the overhead light.

Agnes unbuttoned his coat and flapped the sides. Then, appearing to make up his mind to something, he slipped his coat off, folded it once, and laid it on the floor beside his chair. His shirt was short sleeved, but he rolled the edges anyway, up over his heavy biceps. He caught Doug's eye and winked slightly. Bet didn't miss it.

"Wher're you from?" she asked, her words coming in a rush, as she cocked her head at him.

Agnes grinned and leaned back, posing a little. "A long ways from here."

"Oh, don't go folksy on me. You've got Oklahoma all over you. Is that right? Oklahoma?"

"Yes'm, that's right." He made his grin even bigger.

"Just a country boy." Bet touched her fingers to the round muscle bulging up out of Agnes's bent arm. "A regular hand. I'm from Texas myself."

"Yeah? What part?"

Doug felt warmer and warmer and he couldn't always follow what was being said. He felt a wild "Yippie!" shivered an inch away from realization. He wondered what they'd think if he did yell. The thought made him smile. Agnes and Bet were trying to find some point in the past where their paths might have crossed, some person or street or town between them. Doug turned to Marion.

She was relaxed, sitting two-thirds away from the table, with one arm stretched along the table top holding her glass. Her posture raised one breast and lowered the other and her stomach swelled smoothly. She was full woman, not a girl, though she couldn't have been very old. She was tipping her glass to-and-fro, watching the light play in the amber liquid, but she must have felt his eyes on her, because she turned, and he quickly looked away from her body. Her eyes were light gray, just barely washed with blue, the lashes darker than the iris. Her eyes became part of the warmth inside him, and he smothered the impulse to grab her and swing her around the kitchen.

She spoke to him directly for the first time. "Do you live near here?"

He started to nod, but his head went too far, his chin grazing his chest. He recovered with a start, eyes wide. Then he started laughing.

Marion laughed with him. "You better take it easy. That stuff's not root beer."

Doug heard Agnes's voice going alongside him, Agnes's laugh banging away, and he felt some wild unformed boast rising in himself, but he stifled it. "I'm OK. I'm just fine."

"Cheers then," Marion offered, raising her glass in a half-salute. They drank together.

Bet stood up. Swinging around the table, she stretched over it to turn on a small radio that was sitting with a toaster and a coffee pot. She swung back and picked up her glass, holding it in both hands like a little girl.

Music rushed up, loud, beating. Marion fumbled at the volume control. "The kids," she cautioned, and went to their door to listen.

Bet paid no attention. Snapping her fingers, she swiveled her small hips to the slow, monotonous beat; her skirt dipped and swung around her knees. Agnes stood to meet her and they moved around the kitchen in a languid grind, Agnes pushing the chairs away behind him without missing a step.

Marion stared at them for a moment, biting her knuckle. She moved back to the table and took a quick drink, looking down at Doug.

"What's the matter, baby? Don't you dance?" Then seeing his sudden flush, she made a face of mother's contrition. "I'm sorry. You want to learn?"

Doug stood up, standing as tall as he could, and he felt surer when she had to raise her face to look into his. Her hand was soft and warm as she led him into another room. He saw the dim outline of heavy furniture. She turned on a little amber light, and it spread over the floor leaving the upper walls in shadows. They set their drinks on the lamp table.

"Now we've got a little room," Marion remarked. They stood quietly for a moment, while someone was talking on the radio. The warmth in Doug was beginning to be tinged with a faint sickness. His forehead felt tight, and he could feel his heart working in his throat. He watched Marion and his head felt loose, but he didn't care.

The music started again to the same slow beat, while a hoarse voice dragged over it...

> Baby, how long have I been askin'?
> How long you gonna make me wait?
> Oh, whe-e-e-en, baby, when?

Marion held her arms out, and when he reached for her, she deftly got his hands right, coming into his arms. "Relax," she urged softly. "Just follow the beat."

He circled stiffly, pretending to know even less than he did, the fingers of one hand lightly on her small waist, sensitive to the smooth cloth and the little bulges of her underwear. His other hand perspired in hers. For a moment their feet knocked together and he felt wooden-legged and stupid. Then the beat worked into him, seeping in on the liquor glow.

"That's better," she murmured and pulled closer.

When the music ended he was against her, aware of the warm milky smell of her neck under a trace of old scent. She stepped back and reached for her glass, smiling at him.

Out in the kitchen, Agnes was singing, *Whe-e-e-en, baby, when?*, mimicking the urgent tones of the singer, and Bet said something, her voice low in her throat.

"Here we go again," Marion remarked, with an undertone of irritation. She stared up at Doug, her lids heavy. "Maybe I should give you a rhumba lesson."

Her meaning was clear. She revolved her hips, moving her feet in a small pattern. To cover his confusion, Doug took her glass and gulped from it. A nasty twinge shook him and a thin line of sickness ran up his throat. Then the wild yell came pounding back.

"Do you think I'd be any good at it?" he blurted, and when her face didn't change he added, "The rhumba?"

She grinned. "Sure you would. You'd be great."

The music started again. He reached for Marion. In the amber light, her face glowed beneath her chin, and on the half-ovals of her lower lids. She seemed lovely. They moved around in a simple box step, but to Doug it was a thrilling blur.

Marion put her cheek against his and he was urgently conscious of the warmth of her body; it focused in his groin, expanding there, and he tried to draw away so she wouldn't be conscious of it. But her arm drew him back, and she pressed against him, making a warm soft noise in his ear.

When the music stopped, they didn't separate, but stood swaying in its remembered rhythm. She put both arms around his neck and he bent down, finding her face and her open mouth.

The yell broke free. Silent, but tearing through him.

CHAPTER FIVE

Marion was asleep, her shoulders white above the blankets. Doug felt his head spinning and he knew he was going to throw up soon. Slipping into his pants, he rushed out into the dark house, trying to find the toilet. He threw open the first door he came to and the sudden light seemed to burn his eyes.

He saw a bed, the blankets thrown back off the sheet, and Agnes hunched up over Bet, her thin legs hitched in his, jerking. He was too startled to move, until he saw Bet's eyes, wide and dark in her pale face.

"You little sonofabitch!" she breathed.

He closed the door quickly and his nausea rose furiously. He stumbled through the next door and vomited all over the toilet seat. He had the seat up before it hit him again.

He drank water. It seemed to go down his throat in solid lumps and tasted of his own sickness. After he cleaned up, using a rag he found hanging in the U of the sink drain, he sat on the edge of the claw-footed tub and tried to reconstruct what had happened. It was important to him, and he wanted to remember, but he found that little would come back through the haze of his drunkenness.

He remembered Marion's dress going up over her head, how white her legs were under the black cloth, and the way her bra straps and the elastic band of her pants cut into her flesh. He remembered being both pleased and dismayed at her directness. Then he was fumbling with his shoes, while she said, "Come on to bed, baby." And then a moment later, "Turn out the light."

Reaching for her under the covers, and discovering she still had her underwear on, he remembered his hand very distinctly cupped on the stretched rayon, the heat through the cool cloth. And then she said, "Here, let me."

She made a rising, doubling motion under the covers, and then she was dropping something on the floor, holding the covers around her neck. Then rolling sideways to meet him.

She seemed incredibly soft, softer than he'd ever imagined. Her breath was rushing in his ear, and he loved the shudder in her breath, and it was making him strong....

Now he felt awful. Again he saw Agnes and Bet in their awkward pantomime, and his feeling for Marion drained away, onto the cold bathroom linoleum, into its damp antiseptic air.

Back in the bedroom he straightened out on the side of the bed away from her, but as soon as he closed his eyes, the bed seemed to rise and fall beneath him. He twisted from side to side, trying to sleep, but the pillow was as hot as his feverish cheek. His illness made him lonesome. He rolled over to Marion. She murmured sleepily and put her arm around his neck.

In a moment, he was excited again, but she patted him lightly on the back, and told him, "In the morning."

CHAPTER SIX

In the morning it was grim. Marion's kids woke him up. He opened his eyes to see them standing in front of the bed, a little boy of about five and a younger girl. The boy wore an old pair of khaki pants, too large for him and cut off above the knees. He looked at Doug and ran out of the room, his thin legs stiff.

The bedroom was a mess. He saw his own clothes in an untidy pile. A dresser stood with the drawers open and a pale-blue slip hung down the face of them. Marion's shoes lay on their sides by the door.

The little girl came closer. She stood, looking at Doug and blowing spit bubbles. She was holding a doll with a smashed head, and her belly was a distended curve in her white cotton pants. Her head rolled with interest.

"Mommy," she said tentatively.

Marion rose up in bed, yawning. For a moment her breasts were clear; then she pulled the covers up around her.

"Are you hungry, Dottie? Dottie hungry?"

"Dottie hungry," the little girl repeated with great positiveness and began to hop up and down.

Marion slid out of bed, and keeping her back to Doug, took a robe out of the closet. He was struck with the weight of her hips, contrasting with her waist and the clean line of her back. He wanted to see the rest of her. But she belted the robe around her and gave him a pale grin, before she said, "Come on, Dottie. Mommy fix."

Doug rolled over and closed his eyes. The woman smell was all through the bedclothes and it brought a joy up in him.

He got up, dressed, and went to stand in the kitchen doorway. The kids were at the table, eating bowls of dry cereal. The little boy gave him one furious glance, before he bent his head over his bowl, spooning quickly. His hair was cut very short, the color of dry grass, and his face was pinched by a hard expression; his motions were purposeful and almost adult. He finished his cereal and rushed out, banging the door behind him. The little girl went on humming and jamming her spoon up and down in her bowl.

Marion was fussing with the coffee pot. She saw him, and a hint of the night's fondness came into her face. "Want something to eat?"

He thought he did, until he sat down in front of it. Then his throat refused the cereal, but he could drink the coffee. Marion sat down across from him and gave him a wry smile.

"I've got a beaut myself. Do you suppose those two pigs could have left any of that?"

"If they didn't, I have some money."

"Oh, there'll be some left. They probably went to bed right after we did." She stood up and left the room.

Marion came back with the bottle, still a quarter full. She poured some into his coffee, leaning over him with her hand on his shoulder. Before she left she squeezed his shoulder and brushed his ear with her lips. She spiked her own coffee.

"You're just making a mess," she told her daughter. "Either eat that or go out and play."

Dottie shoved away from the table and started for the door.

"Darn it, Dottie, put some clothes on."

"I can't."

"Sure you can. Aren't you ever going to learn? A big girl like you?"

"I can't. Can't. Can't."

Marion sighed and took Dottie into her own bedroom. Doug sipped the laced coffee and it was flat and metallic-tasting. The first sip recalled the echo of his sickness, but as he forced more of it down he began to wonder how long it would be before Agnes and Bet were up. He thought about getting Marion back into bed.

Dottie ran through the kitchen, wearing a blue playsuit. She stopped to look at him over her shoulder before she ran out the back door, leaving it open.

Marion came back, rubbing her forehead. "Those kids," she said and went to close the door. She took a long drink of her coffee. "That's better. That's much better." She sat down, and began to arrange her hair.

Doug watched her. Her breasts were loose in the thin robe, and he remembered her hands, urgent on his back the night before, and her lips on his ear a few moments ago. He felt bold.

"What happened to our date this morning?"

"What?"

She blushed faintly, and murmured, "The kids—"

"They're playing now," he urged. "You want to, don't you?"

"Give me a chance to find out if I'm alive." Then her lips curved, and she smoothed her hair some more, spreading it out around her face. "You're a regular goat boy, aren't you?"

"Yes'm." He tried to affect Agnes's cocky grin and was pleased to see her grin back.

"Let me fix myself up. I must look like day before yesterday." She finished her coffee and stood up. Leaning over, she opened her mouth on his forehead.

"I'll be right back."

He washed at the kitchen sink, drying on a dish towel, rubbing his teeth with the corner of it. That was the way he'd kept clean in gas-station restrooms, and he thought nothing of it. He combed his hair in a small mirror on the windowsill. Marion's boy ran by below the window, shouting and making whipping motions to the side. He was riding an old branch.

He heard Marion coming, and sat down quickly. She had her hair combed and her mouth was a new pink. Her gray eyes were caught between amusement and affection, she paused in the doorway and smiled at him.

"Come on, baby-brown-eyes."

He caught her inside the bedroom door, grabbing her from behind, sinking his hands into her breasts and his face into her neck.

"Hey!" She broke free. "Can't you wait?"

She locked the bedroom door and pulled down the window shade; the room softened and filled with brown light.

"All right, goat boy—"

He knew right away it was going to be different. She lay openly on the bed, smiling at him as he looked at her, and yet he had the feeling that she was a little shy. Something in the way she held herself.

Then her lips were spreading below his, and her hands were twisting on her arms. Afterwards she helped him, but he was too excited to realize it.

"Like that," she said. And her hips guided him.

At the end he was exultant. He thought he had done it all.

"Oh, that was *nice,*" Marion said, breathing hard.

"I love you," Doug whispered, discovering it as he said it.

"Shush." She put her hand to his mouth.

"But I do. I really do."

"Please. Don't say that."

"It's true. I love you."

She smiled at him. "You're very sweet. You're a candy goat with nice brown eyes, and a soft creamy center and lovely sharp horns—"

"Don't make fun of me, Marion."

She kissed him softly. "I'm not making fun of you. You can be in love with me all this week. But next week I'm going to be five years older than you, with two kids and a husband at sea—OK?"

"I'll love you always." He was furious about the always. It

had to be always.

His tone brought her eyes to his face and she saw his urgent look. "All right. Always—a little bit." Then she rose on one elbow and looked into his eyes. "Was I your first, baby-brown-eyes?"

"Doug, call me Doug. Please."

"I'm sorry, Doug. Was I?"

He started to lie. Then for some reason he didn't. He nodded and looked away, obscurely ashamed.

"Don't feel like that. Everyone has a first time. You were fine."

"It's just that everyone seems to know more about—that sort of thing than I do."

"You were fine," she repeated firmly. "You've been listening to fellows like your buddy in there. They'll tell you they jumped out of their cribs and raped their nurse-maids. They're not half of what they pretend to be, believe me."

He traced the blue veins in her breast with his fingertips. "Can I stay here with you?"

"For awhile. Are you going to work in town?"

"I've got some money," he lied. For a moment his mind left the closed bedroom and he thought of the town, wondering how he could get some money. The police came into his mind, but they seemed remote.

There were noises from beyond the locked door: a chair scraped, and metal clicked on metal.

"They're up," Marion announced, but it didn't seem to mean anything to her. She stretched out on her back and folded her arms behind her head. Doug enjoyed looking at her, thinking of her as his. He put his hand over her breast, the nipple between his fingers. He rolled it gently.

"Don't do that... not now."

"Why not?"

"You know why not."

He grinned, but he didn't stop. She rolled over and put her arms around his neck.

Their door banged. "Mommy? Are you in there, Mommy?" It was the boy's voice, high and strident. "Mommy?"

"What do you want, Butch?"

He ignored her question. "Mommy?"

She sighed and sat up, slipping on her robe. When Doug saw she was going to open the door, he pulled part of the bedspread over himself. As Marion went out, he saw the boy looking around her.

"What is it, Butch?" He heard her voice fading across the room.

CHAPTER SEVEN

"We've got to think about some money," Agnes said, the first time they were alone.

"I know it."

"And we've got to be a damn sight more careful than we were last night."

Doug winced. "There's always that chance. It might have been one of us."

But Agnes hadn't been thinking of Billy. He held up his hand, stopping Doug. "Just so we don't end up with a few bucks. We've got to make it. One way or another."

"We'll make it," Doug said, more firmly than he felt.

Agnes was cleaned up. He'd shaved, and had something on his hair that darkened it and made it lay close to his head. He looked good, except the clothes from the cleaners were already wrinkled. Doug looked down at his own pants. The crease was gone.

"Did you make out?" Agnes asked.

"Sure."

"Puts that jail a long way behind us, huh?"

Agnes had lowered his voice on the word "jail," but Doug still looked around quickly. They were alone in the living room. The same room where he'd danced with Marion, but it seemed different in the daylight. The marks of the children were all over it, their handprints and scuffs; the leg of a fuzzy toy protruded from under the sofa.

The girls were in the back, doing something. A yipping noise came from outside, where Marion's boy was pursuing Indians with an imaginary partner called Old Joe.

Agnes lounged on the sofa, his feet crossed on the arm. He was battling a tassled lamp pulled above his head, keeping it going around, rattling on the glass base. Doug walked over and looked into the unfinished wood bookcase: a Bible, a pocket dictionary, one volume of a child's pictorial encyclopedia, and two romances by Louise Corelli. The edges were all yellowed by the sun. Most of the bookcase was stuffed with picture magazines and a ragged pile of comic books.

"How about that money of yours?" he heard Agnes ask. He heard the sofa creak and he knew Agnes was sitting up, but he didn't turn around. He stared at the book covers.

"I'm not sure I remember where it is."

"What the hell? Haven't you got any idea? You must remember something—"

"No—it was dark when I hid it."

Agnes slapped the arm of the sofa, and dust puffed up through his fingers. "I wish I had a gun. I'd sure jack some money out of this town in a hurry."

"We don't need a gun. We'll find something tonight."

"Yeah? You tell me where, buddy?"

Doug made a spreading gesture. "Somewhere around here."

"We sure as hell better. These broads ain't going to keep us. They ain't that bad off. This bitch I'm shagging is already hinting around about how she's got a watch in hock. And you know what that means."

Doug smiled as he said, "Marion thinks we're going to work."

"Fat chance!"

"In a way it's too bad we can't."

"Nuts! What would we do? Sweep up? Wash dishes?"

"I don't know. There ought to be something we could do—but I guess it doesn't matter anyway."

"We'll work tonight. That's enough work for me."

Agnes stretched out on the sofa again. In a moment he had the lamp pull spinning. Doug took some magazines to the chair that matched the sofa. He was leafing through an old copy of *Life* when Bet came in. He looked up, ready to smile at her, but she ignored him and perched on the sofa arm above Agnes's head.

"Didn't you get enough sleep last night?" Her voice was edged. The daylight was unfriendly to her. Her skin was pale and her mouth seemed very red.

"I was born tired," Agnes replied, rolling over so he could look at her.

She arched a little under his inspection, perhaps aware that she wasn't looking her best. She sat with her legs crossed and her hip cocked; a sharp bone was outlining her pedal pushers. She had her hair in pins, under a scarf.

"Well?" she asked, inviting a compliment.

Agnes rolled back and went on flicking the tassle with his forefinger, until she reached over and stopped it.

"You'll break that."

"I'm sorry, mommy."

"Oh, can it. What are we going to do? Lay around here all day?" She put her fingers on Agnes's mouth and he nipped them.

"I don't know. What do you want to do?"

"Anything's better than poking around the house all day. I get so tired of those brats of Marion's. Let's go out. I'll show you where that place is."

Doug saw an opaque look come into Agnes's eyes. "What place?" he asked quietly.

"You know. Where my watch is."

"I told you about that, didn't I?"

"Yes, but I thought I could show you where it is now, and then you could—you know—"

Agnes didn't answer and after a moment, Bet reached over
and took him by the arm. "Please, baby, let's go out. I get
bitchy just sitting around here."

"All right. All right. What about a show? Is there one around
here?"

"About five or six blocks."

"Want to go?"

"Sure. That's great." Bet stood up and started out. "I'll get
my coat."

When she was out of the room, Agnes shook his head, and
blew his breath out. "She's wild—real wild. How's yours?"

Doug didn't answer. He just shrugged and smiled. Agnes
laughed. "You like her, huh?"

Doug changed the subject.

"You think it's safe out now?"

Agnes came over and squatted down in front of him, tapping
his knee. "It's safer, and she'll make nice camouflage, but let
me tell you something—this town ain't ever going to be safe,
or this state either as far as that goes. When this gets to be a
drag we'll steal a car and cut out."

Doug found he was no longer looking forward to going with
Agnes. He wanted to stay with Marion. He made a half-nod,
face quiet.

CHAPTER EIGHT

They had trouble getting away from the house that evening.
Bet, acting as if she were jealous, asked some awkward questions, her brown eyes unexpectedly sharp. Agnes tried to
sweet-talk her, but she just looked at him and said, "Sure,
sure."

But Marion handed Doug a key and told him to be careful
not to wake the kids when he came in. He drew her aside and
kissed her, and her hands came up to the back of his neck. She
brushed up his long hair and murmured that he needed a hair-

cut. He promised to get one, feeling a strange sweetness looking into her face.

When they were alone on the sidewalk, Agnes said, "Damned if you haven't got that broad trained already. I should have hung on to her. At least there's something there to get hold of."

Doug didn't answer. He rejected Agnes's notion that he could have had Marion so easily. The idea was obscene and painful.

Then Agnes was showing him something in his hand, and as he turned to look, a knife blade sprang out with a sharp click.

"Just in case we have trouble tonight," Agnes explained, making a sudden deft lunge with the knife. "I picked it up this afternoon."

They started out as carefully as they had the first night, keeping to the shadows, avoiding the pools thrown by the streetlights, and in a few hours they were on their way back with over six hundred dollars.

Doug had been more surprised than Agnes, but he was careful not to show it. Within fifteen minutes of entering a furniture store, they'd turned up the money in a small metal cabinet.

Agnes had insisted on spending some of it immediately, and they came back carrying two fifths of Grand Dad, a carton of cigarettes, and some packages of mixed nuts and dried salmon. Agnes had asked for one of everything he saw.

He swung the bottles in a paper bag and told Doug, "I was beginning to think you were conning me about getting money like that. But you sure as hell wasn't. This puts us in good shape. You know that?"

Doug was full of excited pleasure. He thought of a lot of things he wanted to buy for Marion. Then she wouldn't smile at him as if he were a child.

The house was dark, and Agnes lit a match so they could find their way through the garage. Doug saw the flame swimming on the bottles. They depressed him, because in his imagination each bottle represented a man, a different man, bringing his liquor as they had and finding his way to bed.

Then he was sure it was Bet and the other girl who were responsible for the bottles.

Agnes wanted to sit up and drink and talk. He was still wound up with the tension he'd generated crouched in the dark store. While Doug peeked in Marion's room, assuring himself with the dim outline of her hips, Agnes counted the money out on the kitchen table. He smoothed out the bills and stacked them. He made piles of halves and quarters—with a sudden arrogance they'd ignored anything smaller—and when Doug sat down across from him, he flipped the halves over like a gambler with chips.

"Beats twenty bucks all hollow."

"That was nothing," Doug said. "Just eating money."

They drank out of glasses still faintly tinged with milk, probably from the kids' dinner. The single light made a circle from above the table, catching the sun-streaks in Agnes's hair, glinting on the sides of the coins, and to Doug the scene at the table with the money between them seemed real and important. He swirled his drink and looked at it as he'd seen people do in the movies.

"Where'd you go this afternoon?" he said casually.

"That same show. Must be the only one out this way. I bet I know those goddam pictures by heart."

"There's three shows downtown. Two big ones right across the street from each other and another down the way."

"There could be a hundred downtown and all free—a lot of good it does us." Agnes pushed his share of the money together and started putting it in his pocket. "I'm not going to last much longer here. And that's for damn sure. This is just another jail, and I hate being cooped up."

"What about Bet?"

"What about her?"

"Well, would you want to go without her?"

"There's ten like her in any bar you go in. You'll see. For Christ's sake, don't go and get lovesick on me."

Doug thought, I don't have to go. He'll go back home— he's probably got buddies there. Having found the money seemed to free him from Agnes. He'd done what he said he could.

Agnes leaned forward, asking urgently, "How about it? You want to cut out tomorrow?" He lowered his voice. "These broads probably have some loot around here. We'll clean them out too."

Doug shoved his chair back. "No."

"What?"

"I said no. We've got enough money."

"Oh, crap!"

"No kidding. I mean it, Ernie."

"OK. All right. Let them keep their few dollars. I still want to cut out tomorrow."

"I don't know. Why not wait a while longer?"

"What for? Tomorrow makes three days. The road'll be clear tomorrow night. Come on, buddy, how about it?"

Doug looked directly into Agnes's eyes. He saw that they were soft and anxious like a young dog's, and the thought came to him that Agnes wouldn't leave without him. It didn't matter then what he said.

"Maybe. We don't have to decide right now." Then because being in control was so new to him he found it almost frightening, he added, "Why don't we talk about it tomorrow?"

He was a little drunk by the time he went to bed. He didn't try to keep from blundering in the dark, hoping Marion would wake up. But she slept soundly, her face shadowed under one arm. As he slid in beside her, she turned to him in her sleep.

CHAPTER NINE

Out on the highway, in a narrow ravine three miles from town, Huey stopped a car and raked the interior with his flash.

"Sorry, folks." He motioned them on.

He stepped back to the prowl car angled on the roadside. Pete handed him a thermos-top full of coffee and remarked, "It doesn't look like they're coming out."

Huey turned his heavy face down the highway—more lights showed on a crest half a mile away.

"It sure as hell doesn't." He shrugged and sipped the coffee. "I wouldn't have credited them with enough sense to hide out."

Pete studied the darkness around them, where the underbrush grew almost to the sides of the road. "What makes you so sure they're hiding? They could walk right by us out here. They could be fifty feet away right now. We'd never know it."

"Nuts! Those kind don't walk. They ride. You wait and see. They're hiding out; we'll probably catch them in town."

"If we catch them. You think they'll keep us at it out here?"

"No, the captain'll probably pull the block in the morning."

"You think so?"

"Pretty certain," Huey said as he stepped out of the highway, signaling the approaching car with his flash. He brushed his holster flap to see if his gun was free.

CHAPTER TEN

Doug was alone in the house. Marion's boy was playing somewhere outside and Doug was supposed to be keeping an eye on him, but the kid made him uncomfortable, reminding him of Marion's husband somewhere on the sea—but maybe not on the sea, maybe on a bus coming towards them....

Agnes had made the mistake of letting Bet see his money, and she'd wheedled him into going out. Doug had watched the whole thing and he was sure Agnes had intended Bet to see the money. He didn't understand the contradiction that seemed to imply. Agnes whispered to him, "There's no sense getting these broads mad at us."

As soon as they were out of the house, Doug went to Marion's room, but he found her putting her coat on. She had to take Dottie to the clinic for some shots, and he decided to wait. He didn't want to take her shopping with the kids along.

He killed time posing in front of the bedroom mirror. He posed with a glass of whiskey like the ad with the butler hovering deferentially in the background, and then he posed by the side of his plane, having broken some world's record, and he put Marion a little to the side so she could admire him.

"What're you doing in my mommy's bedroom?"

The boy startled him, appearing suddenly in the lower corner of the mirror. He turned around feeling foolish.

"It's all right. She told me I could."

"It's not all right! It's not all right!" The boy ran out, shaking his head wildly.

Doug followed him and found him with his back turned, picking at the pile of comic books. "Are those yours?" Doug asked, hoping to make some kind of easy talk.

The boy whirled and looked up, his eyes bleak. "You won't be here when my daddy comes home. My daddy'll make you go away." He ran out of the room, leaving Doug strangely upset.

He's a kid, he thought, but the thought didn't help, because it was the boy's youth that drove the rejection home and left him without any defense against it. He could see himself as he must appear in the boy's world, a big strange monster, and he recognized the boy's courage and knew it for better than his own.

He put his glass aside. Now it seemed foolish, drinking alone in an empty house. He sat down and stared at the knuckles of his hands, and through his hands at the faded geometry woven into the rug. He smoothed the nap with the sole of his dirty shoe, and for a moment his mind opened. The thing with the boy caused the present to become transparent, and the future trembled in front of him. What chance did he have to stay with Marion? How long could it last? A few weeks before, of all the things moving against them, one hit. Which one? Would it matter? The husband at sea, the police, or the five years between them that nothing could ever erase—

He heard someone at the back door, and crossed quickly towards the kitchen, hoping for Marion. A strange girl was pouring whiskey into one of the glasses left on the table.

"Hi," she said, without pausing. Jinx, he thought. It must be. A cloth overnight bag was sitting on a chair, and she had an extra coat over her arm. He tried to see what it was Bet disliked so much. He recalled the exact tone of malice in Bet's voice, and it surprised him now, because Jinx seemed very much like Bet. *Used* was the expression that occurred to him.

Jinx winked at him, topped the glass and swallowed deeply. She smiled and blew her breath in a soft, fat whistle.

"I've been dreaming of that. That and a few other things." She touched the label with her finger and he noticed the chipped nail polish. "Grandpop, too. Things must be looking up around here. Who's springing?"

"I bought it."

She looked him over deliberately and he couldn't miss the humor in her eyes. "Who do you belong to?"

"No one," he mumbled.

"Well, there's nothing wrong with your liquor. Let's take it in the other room and see if we can make a dent in it."

She passed close to him and he saw that her skirt was wrinkled and her hair dull. When she smiled, her large teeth forced her lip back, and they weren't too clean, but her eyes were lively and her voice brash and friendly. He followed her into the living room and watched, feeling awkward, while she kicked off her shoes and sat down on the rug, placing the bottle in front of her.

"Well, come on. Aren't you sociable? What's been going on around here?"

"Not much." He squatted down across from her. "I've only been here a few days."

"Oh? Did they mention me? Jinx?"

"Well, they were expecting you back. That's all."

"I'll bet. Do you know if Roy's been here?"

"No one's been here except Ernie and me."

"Who's Ernie?"

"My partner."

"Oh. Look, angel, get me the phone will you?"

The phone was closer to her than it was to him, but he got up and handed it to her. She leaned back on the front of the sofa and cradled the phone in her lap while she dialed.

"You got a cig, angel?"

He started to shake his head, then he remembered the carton Agnes had bought the night before. He found them on Bet's dresser, already faintly dusted with powder.

He tore the top of the pack, trying to appear as if he weren't listening. She was asking for someone named Roy. On impulse Doug lit two cigarettes. He handed her one of them and she gave him a quick smile, her teeth showing for an ugly moment.

He watched her face. With her mouth closed she looked younger than Bet or Marion, and, as always, he was conscious of her body, trying to read its contours beneath her clothes.

She leaned her head back into the sofa seat, making a long line of her neck. It throbbed gently as she spoke. "Haven't you any idea where he is?" After a moment she frowned and slammed the phone down.

"The sonofabitch. He knew I was due out."

She was quiet for the space between two drinks, head down, her fingers tapping against her elbow; then she threw her head up.

"You got a name?" she asked.

"Doug."

"No kidding? I used to know a kid by that name. He was in my class at school—a hell of a sweet guy. He didn't have any eyes for me though."

She paused, looking inside herself, and for a moment he saw another face behind the one she wore. Then it faded away and she pulled at her drink.

"Well, come on—" The amusement was back in her eyes. "Say something. This is my homecoming party. Aren't you going to help me celebrate?"

"Marion ought to be home soon. She had to take Dottie to the clinic."

"Where's Butch?"

"He's outside somewhere."

"Good place for him. I hope he drowns himself. And where's her majesty, Queen Bet?"

"Out with Ernie."

"Oh? What's going on there?"

"I don't know. Nothing, I guess."

"You sure *don't* know, then. How's old's this Ernie?"

"He's older than me."

Jinx nodded as if she were guessing something, tipping the bottle over her glass. He emptied his own glass and held it over, beginning to feel that now almost familiar warmth.

"I didn't expect this," Jinx said, indicating the bottle of Grand Dad. "I'd have settled for a beer. Well, here's to extinction."

Someone knocked on the front door, and Jinx was up, smoothing her skirt over her legs. She threw the door open and stepped back.

"Oh, it's you, Arnie." Her voice was toneless.

"Jinxie. When'd you get back?"

"Just a few minutes ago."

"What's the matter? You don't sound very happy about it."

"It's nothing. I was kind of hoping it was Roy. You haven't seen him, have you? Well, you might as well come in."

Jinx moved away from the door, turning her back on the

short man who entered. Doug recognized him. He was the man who'd danced with Marion at the bar. He wasn't drunk now, but he was wearing the same clothes, plus an old gray hat with a feather in the band.

"I've only got a minute. Is Marion here?" He shifted his feet and looked around as if he expected to see through the walls.

Jinx answered, "The kid here says Marion went over to the clinic."

"Yeah? Do you know when she'll be back?"

"No," Doug answered shortly, turning away. He remembered this man's loose foolish mouth on Marion's neck.

"Have a drink, Arnie." Jinx's voice was bright again. "I'm giving a little party."

Arnie shook his head with an elaborate sour look. "I'm cutting down." He took his hat off.

Jinx grinned at the hat in his hand and sat down, folding her legs under her. Her skirt billowed and her thighs flashed.

"Cut down tomorrow. Today's a holiday. Independence Day."

"I really shouldn't. I got to get home."

"See if you can find another glass, will you, Doug?"

In the kitchen he looked through a cloudy glass and decided not to wash it. It was good enough for Arnie.

Coming back, he heard Jinx talking in a coaxing voice. "You better stick around, Arnie. I got something special for you. Just for friendlies, too."

He saw Jinx showing Arnie her big front teeth in a grin that was half taunt and half invitation, and Arnie was smiling with a nervous shyness.

"I'd like to. Jinx—you know I would. But Lucy—"

"Lucy can't do what I can do."

Arnie made his sour face again. "Lucy can't do much of anything—or won't. However it is, it comes out the same."

"Then we've got a date?" Jinx suggested, rocking back and forth from the waist, her arms crossed under her breasts, pushing them up. She watched Arnie's eyes cross hers and skitter away. Her smile deepened.

Doug handed her the glass, and Arnie brushed the back of his hand against his nose, watching her pour for him.

She leaned towards him with the glass.

"Nice old Arnie. How about it?"

Arnie took a couple of hurried gulps and shook his shoulders, letting the liquor settle into him. Then, looking at Jinx's mouth, he said carefully, "I'm sorry as hell, Jinx, but I've got to get going. You know how it is."

"No," Jinx asked coldly, "How is it? Tell me how it is."

Arnie stood up, setting his glass on the table, still with a half inch of amber liquid in it. He put his hat on.

"Thanks for the drink. I'm glad you're back, and I'll be around to see you in a couple of days." He smiled hopefully. "If you want to keep that offer open."

"It just went up, Arnie. Everything's going up, you know."

He shrugged and started to leave with a kind of weary dignity, pausing at the door to ask, "Will you tell Marion I dropped by?"

Jinx didn't answer, didn't move until the door closed. Then she snatched out a cigarette and began to fumble with a book of paper matches. She struck the matches so hard, it lit with a distinct "pop," and the flare shadowed a nest of wrinkles in her forehead. She threw the match at an ashtray, missing it.

"If I wasn't such a bitch, I'd probably be bawling. I can't even give it away." She turned to Doug. "Do I have a wart on my nose or something?"

He picked the match up and dropped it in the tray.

"No, you look all right." He couldn't think of anything else.

"Well, that's a gracious little speech. I can see you know a lot about women."

He forced his mouth to move. "What should I have said?"

"Oh, I don't know. Something nice. Don't you see anything nice about me?"

"Sure."

"Then what is it?"

He wanted to say, I like the way your ass moves when you walk. That's what Agnes would have said, and he knew she would laugh. He could almost hear her—

"I like your eyes."

"My eyes?" She closed them quickly and asked, "What color are they?"

"What?" he stalled.

"What—color—are—my—eyes?"

"Brown," he guessed.

Then she did laugh and leaned over to him. "Do they look brown?"

Her eyes were almost hazel, very light around the pupil, and out of the corners the tiny veins grew like a delicate plant. He was close enough to smell the whiskey swimming on her breath, but he didn't mind, because her eyes hit him with exactly the same impact Marion's had, and remembering what had followed, what he had found of himself in Marion, some obstruction in his spirit fractured and let him stay as he was, deliberately looking into her eyes, holding up a kind of dare.

She looked away first, covering herself by taking another drink. "How old are you, anyway?"

"What difference does that make? That's all I've been hearing. Everyone wants to know how old I am. Well, I'm old enough to be on my own. I'm old enough to take care of myself. So what does that mean?"

He had a crazy impulse to pull the money out of his pocket and show it to her. His hand even moved, but he turned it into an aimless gesture.

"I must have hit a sore spot. That's the most you've said since I got home."

"I get tired of being treated like a damned baby."

"Then why do you act like one? You mumble and look everywhere but at me."

"I looked. You just didn't see me."

"I don't mind you looking. I don't think any woman minds being looked at. You remember that."

"I will," he said, and as he said it he let his eyes go over her slowly.

She laughed with her head thrown back, and against his will his eyes went to her teeth. "You might at that," she said, shifting her legs straight out in front of her. She looked at him with deliberate provocation.

She'd put her legs right next to where his hand was resting on the rug, and it was easy for him to put it between her knees. She turned her feet out, letting his hand slip in along her thigh, finding the flesh above the top of her stocking. His hand started to caress her almost by itself.

Jinx leaned towards him, her eyes half-closed. "You sure you don't belong to Marion?"

He shook his head, sliding his hand deeper.

"Wait a minute, angel. I'll be right back." She stood up, settling her skirt. "I'll be right back," she repeated at the door.

He rolled over on his stomach and flexed his hips, wondering if she'd be different. He knew he'd please her, but he wondered how he'd feel. He remembered the big soft hammer that hit him with Marion—hit him and hit him.

He met Jinx on his knees, reaching for her hand, and pulling her down beside him. Her hand was cool, still a little damp, and when he kissed her, her mouth tasted of toothpaste. He kissed her twice, and she made a little noise of pleasure, pressing against him. He loosened her blouse and ran his hands up her back until he found the fastener on her bra. She threw her shoulders back so he could cope with the fastener, and her breasts came loose under her blouse. He lifted them with his hands, bending her back.

"You want to go to the bedroom?" he asked.

"This is fine," she said slowly, letting her head roll. "This is just fine."

He pulled her skirt up around her hips, noticing how her white legs flattened on the rug. That was the last image he retained.

He was aware of her face somewhere under his, aware that

she was saying something, and that the tone of her voice was wrong.

He spent himself in a brief spasm almost like pain. He stopped, becoming conscious of her skirt bunched underneath him. There was a moment of complete silence, then the yammering of the radio filled in his head like dirty water.

"All right, hotshot. Get off me."

He rolled to the side, sick with humiliation. He sensed her beside him, then heard her bitter murmur. "High and dry."

"I could try again in a little while."

"Big deal!"

He felt a sudden stringing impulse to smash her in the belly—his arm even tensed, but that was as far as he could go. The impulse shattered and dribbled through him.

He didn't hear the door, only a quickly rising murmur of voices, ending in an amused snort. He sat up to see Bet in the kitchen door. Agnes's face moved above her shoulder. He was smiling.

Bet's laugh was pleased and nasty. "Well, here's little Jinx in her most familiar pose. Welcome home. I didn't know you went in for child-molesting."

Jinx pulled her skirt down, but without haste, and sitting up, she began to fasten her bra. "He's no child," she said. "He may look like it, but he doesn't act like it."

And Doug understood that she was only pretending to build him up to rob Bet of her spite, and even knowing this he could still feel pleased.

"This is going to gas Marion. Oh, she'll just love this." Bet's voice shimmered with malice. "She's soft on this kid."

Jinx's eyes were on him, hard. "I thought you told me you weren't with Marion?"

"You asked me if I belonged to her."

"You knew what I meant." When he could make no further answer, she shook her head in disgust. "There isn't much that doesn't go in this house, but one thing we don't do is trade off." She turned back to Bet. "I didn't know."

Agnes stepped forward, grinning. "You're just rootin' 'n' snortin', ain't you, buddy?"

Jinx stood up, studying Agnes. "What's your name?" she asked in a completely different voice.

Agnes looked puzzled by her tone. "Ernie. Why?"

"Ernie what?"

He started to make some answer, but Jinx cut him off, almost shouting at Bet, "You damn fool. Are you out of your head? You know who this guy is?"

"Wait a—"

"He broke out of jail. And this one too, probably. Every cop in town's looking for them."

Bet's face opened briefly in amazement, then sealed into a stony hostility. "I knew something was wrong with them," she said slowly. "They were broke yesterday. Then last night they went out for a few hours and now they're loaded. You must be right."

"I know I am." Jinx pointed at Agnes. "I saw his picture this morning when I checked out. They've got it on a bulletin board in the sheriff's office—"

"What's the idea?" Bet demanded. "What kind of trouble are you trying to get me into?"

At the direct question, Agnes shifted into some kind of action. He moved between them warily, balancing his weight on his spread legs.

"Take it easy. No one knows we're here."

"Take it easy!" Bet repeated scornfully. "Why, you cheap bastard! Why should I do anything for you?"

"To keep from getting your neck broke. How's that for a reason?"

"You won't touch me. If you do, the minute you turn your back, I'll call the police."

Agnes slapped her so hard she sat down, folding up with her legs sprawling.

"Call!" he shouted at her. "Go on, call! See what you get."

No one moved. Bet held her cheek, her mouth working

soundlessly.

Then Jinx edged away from Agnes until she was near a door. She was pale, but when she spoke her voice was level. "You two better get out of here. Out of here, and out of town."

"We're doing all right," Agnes muttered, rubbing his hands on the sides of his pants.

Bet took her hand away from her cheek. A red welt ran clear around to behind her ear. "I hope they catch him. I hope they blow his goddam head off."

Doug was confused and afraid of the emotions that were alive in the room. He just wanted to get out of the house.

"Let's go," he said.

"They're not running me off," Agnes shouted, shaking his head like an angry animal. "That bitch'll be on the phone the minute we step out the door."

"That's true any time you leave," Jinx said, still evenly. "You can't stay here forever."

"Let's go, Ernie," Doug pleaded.

Agnes stared down at Bet, scouring his fist into the palm of his hand. "You're nothing," he told her. "Just plain nothing. Did you think I was going to get you a lot of stuff, just 'cause you gave me some of your tired ass?"

Doug sensed that Agnes was lashing out blindly, trying to hurt Bet as much as he could, and he felt a flood of similar resentment against Jinx. He looked at her; her hair was still rumpled from the brief and humiliating thing they had done on the rug. Buck-tooth bitch, he thought, seizing gladly on her most prominent defect. He thought, This is how Ernie must feel. Then fear came crowding back.

"Come on, Ernie."

"OK. To hell with them."

Agnes scooped the phone up from where it was still lying on the floor, jerked it out of the wall, and threw it over beside Bet. The receiver jarred loose and cracked her on the knee.

"Now call," he told her. "Come on, Doug. Let's get out of here."

CHAPTER ELEVEN

They met Marion coming up the sidewalk. Doug caught sight of her blue coat and winced, but it was too late to turn around and go the other way. Dottie was straining at her hand, hopping out in an arc the length of her mother's arm. Marion stopped and smiled, but Agnes brushed by her without a word.

"What's the matter with him?" she asked Doug.

"Nothing—he had a fight with Bet. I got to go for awhile. I'll be right back."

She smiled archly. "See that you do." Then seeing that he was already edging around her, looking after Agnes, she gave him a real smile and said, "Hurry back."

"I will. I'll be right back."

His eyes slid away from hers and he ran after Agnes, remembering the freshness of her face against the blue of her collar, her fond and untroubled eyes; then he was alongside Agnes.

"What're we going to do now?"

Agnes turned to him, and he saw that the hard look was in Agnes's eyes—he knew it now—a depthless, almost empty surface, like the opaque blue marbles he used to steal in the dime store.

"Don't sweat it," Agnes said shortly. "I told you last night I was ready to move on. I just don't want no bitch running me off."

"You think she'll call the police?"

"Hell no! She'll be scared to go near a phone for weeks."

Agnes set a hard pace, almost running, stitching back and forth, up one block and down the next, moving out of the neighborhood the quickest way. Down one of the side streets they were passing, Doug saw the beer sign with the painted NED'S. He didn't feel anything. Marion seemed like someone he'd read about in a book.

The sky was pale with the late afternoon, stained a remote gray, the color of old newspapers, and it laid the same neutral glaze over everything—the houses and the set faces of the few people they passed on the sidewalk. Whenever anyone came towards them, Agnes drew his head into his collar, looking at his feet, until they passed by.

At a busier street, Agnes paused, looking both ways, still guarding his face in the curve of his hunched shoulders. Doug noticed a persistent muscle jumping in his cheek. Tension. He felt it himself.

The edges of the sky were grayer, the shadows settling. As he turned back to Agnes, a gust of wind stirred his pants cuff. Agnes felt it too. He jammed his hands into his pockets, still looking around.

Doug waited. Agnes would decide on something. He felt exposed on the street corner, but it wasn't danger he felt as much as guilt. Guilt that anyone who saw him would read in his face as if his head were turned inside out, the guilt festering in plain sight. The money in his pocket seemed worthless. Almost a burden.

Then the feeling slipped away as Agnes picked a new direction and they were moving again.

"We could try hitchhiking," Doug suggested.

"We could do worse," Agnes agreed, "but the wrong guy might pick us up. Let's find a car we can steal. There's got to be a car lot around here somewhere."

But they didn't find one. They continued, deeper into the town, Agnes near the curb looking into the parked cars in the vain hope that someone might have forgotten their keys, until ahead of them they saw the few taller buildings that marked the beginning of the downtown area. Lights were already on in some of them, thin yellow squares in the gathering twilight. A vivid scarlet rope circled one building, and electric blue letters popped on and off.

Agnes had him by the arm in a biting grip, puffing him roughly. "Don't look! The heat's across the street."

Doug couldn't keep from looking. Automatically his head swiveled and in the scattered traffic he saw the white side and the black knobbed searchlights, moving slowly.

Then, like Agnes, he pretended to be passionately interested in something in a store window. A sign hit him: *Vigoro Makes Your Garden Grow*. And the silly rhyme bounced in his head like a ball—*garden-grow, garden-grow, garden-grow*....

Agnes nudged him sharply. "Let's get out of here."

They ran openly. The police seemed real again for the first time since the night they'd caught Billy—was that only two nights ago? Some of the feeling of that frightened, guilty retreat came to him again. Then the town had seemed neutral, unconcerned with them, but now it seemed hostile. The lights were coming on to expose them; cars slowed to watch them; empty windows filled with eyes, and shoe clerks walking home to dinner became plainclothesmen.

Doug wanted to hide, go under somewhere and wait it out, but Agnes had the wind up too and Agnes couldn't sit still from anxiety. He had to try something.

They started on a wide circle, skirting the center of town, while Agnes tried the doors of the older cars they passed. They had to pass up several because there was too much light and activity around them, too much chance of someone spotting them in the middle of the clumsy business of trying to find the right wires.

Then, on a quiet side street, they found an old model Dodge.

"This is it," Agnes exclaimed. "I've seen Billy wire these."

He flicked his knife open and slid across the seat, feeling under the dash. Doug stood with his hand on the open door, looking back and forth between Agnes and the street. They were in front of a block-long funeral parlor surrounded by lawns.

Agnes hit the starter, but it wouldn't catch. The cold motor labored off the battery. He swore and jerked the wires around, squinting over them in the bad light.

"Strike a match! How the hell am I supposed to see what I'm doing?"

"I don't have any."

"Here—for crissake!"

He got a match going and held it cupped over Agnes's hands. Suddenly the windshield silvered. He saw two headlights bearing directly on him. He slapped Agnes hard on the shoulder, and started running, crouched down, keeping the old Dodge between him and the approaching lights. He heard Agnes on the pavement behind him and started on an angle across the lawn, heading for a corner of the building.

Shouting. A car door slammed.

The blue shadows on the far side of the mortuary closed around him. He ran, hardly aware of himself or the situation, twisting through some small trees, over a hedge and down a narrow passage between the main building and a garage. He could see a street down there. A bus passed as he ran towards it, the bright squares flicking across the narrow opening, idle eyes watching the passing street. He heard Agnes on his heels and slowed enough to let him take the lead.

"Cops?"

Agnes grunted. His features twisted as he strained around to look over his shoulder.

They hit the sidewalk just as a prowl car was turning the corner above them, its spotlight licking around like an excited tongue.

"There's more!"

They made it halfway down the next block, but the rising whine of a siren told them they'd been spotted. They went over fences, in and out of several inner courts, tipping things over, blundering in their haste.

Then they dropped into a small parking lot. A man was climbing into a panel truck with SAM THE TELEVISION MAN lettered on the side. He paused with his foot in the cab and turned to look at them. When Agnes started towards him, he slid in and tried to slam the door, but Agnes caught it.

Doug saw the dull glint of the knife. He stopped, breathing hard, instantly opposed to what Agnes was doing. Over the distant roaring of his own breath, he heard the violence in Agnes's voice.

"Just keep still, mister. You're going to take us for a drive."

The man had a small face and a cocky ruff of hair. He tugged feebly away from Agnes's hand clamped on his leather lapel, and his eyes wavered between the knife poised under his chin and Agnes's face. His mouth opened, but he only made a low sound deep in his throat.

"You understand?"

The man nodded his head above the knife point.

Anges pulled the seat forward, pushing the driver against the steering wheel, and motioned Doug in with the knife. He squeezed past the seat, almost stumbling on some chains. A single television set, covered with a furniture blanket, was in the back, and he crouched beside it, watching Agnes position himself behind the driver. Agnes would be hidden from the street, but the driver only had to turn his head to see the knife an inch from his neck.

"All right. Get started."

The man was shaking so badly he stalled the motor twice trying to get it into gear, and Agnes snarled at him, on the edge of hysteria. Then the truck started off, jerking, and through the windshield Doug saw the wall sweep away and the street appear.

"Turn the goddam lights on."

The street rushed up and turned as the windows of a restaurant went by, the people sitting quietly at the white tables. Agnes ducked his head as a prowl car passed, its red light pulsing. Doug turned to follow it, but the back doors of the truck were solid.

"Keep going," Agnes instructed. "Straight out of town. And take the shortest way."

A tense silence held them for a few minutes. Doug felt blind in the back of the truck. His eyes never left the windshield and each new pair of headlights left him breathless. He continued to react even when he knew they were safe on the outskirts of town. The blocks were less solid: single buildings standing alone, single streetlights rising and falling behind them.

Agnes shifted and glanced back. "Looks like we're out of that."

"For now, anyway."

"We're out of it. We'll keep going."

"Like this?"

"No! Hell, no! We're going to get out and start walking while this clown busts his britches trying to find the nearest cop."

"What are you going to do with me, boys?"

The man's voice came up in a painful quaver. Doug saw his profile etched in the light from the dash, before Agnes's rising back cut it off as he climbed into the front seat.

"You just keep driving. You'll come out all right."

Doug moved to the front. He watched the face of their hostage and found the naked fear there indecent. He had to look away. Dangling from a sun-guard above his head was a dime-store rabbit's foot. The speedometer was twitching straight up, around fifty. He saw that Agnes still held his knife at the man's side.

A road sign washed up in the headlights, a stark white square: CARSTENS 30 MILES.

"Did you see that?" Doug asked.

"What?"

"The next town. It's only thirty miles away."

"We're not stopping."

"It's a nice town."

"Sure, I know. And you've got some money hid there. Is that it? How much of a duck do you think I am?"

Agnes said this without looking at him, almost indifferently, and after a pause he added, "I'm going home. I don't care what you do."

Doug felt his face grow hot. He opened his mouth to make some explanation, but his tongue was an ugly mass. There

was no explanation, except more lies. He was caught; the lie
about the money had slapped him down, destroying the very
thing he'd hoped to build with it. And the thought that he
tried to hold on to was that it was so senseless. He'd made the
money for them, in spite of the lie, so he hadn't needed it any
more than he had needed Jinx when he had Marion, and Jinx
had gone as sour and empty as the hidden money. It was all of
a piece.

He remembered that the night before he hadn't cared what
Agnes thought, or what he did, or where he went. He tried to
recall that feeling, but it only seemed strange that he could
have ever felt so certain. He did care, but he also knew that
he'd had enough of what they were doing.

Now he wanted out of the truck, away from the frightened
driver, and whatever it was Agnes was planning. In the lights
of a passing car he saw a handle on the inside of the back
doors. He decided to slip out at the first stop sign and find
some way back to Marion.

The brakes caught. He heard the tires shriek, and felt himself
thrown against the back of the seat. He heard Agnes, his voice
strangely low. "Keep driving. Goddam you, go on through."

Ahead, picked out in their lights, a county car was sitting
across the road, and at its hood an anonymous deputy was
waving a flash in a long arc. Doug realized they were trapped.
The driver seemed frozen.

Agnes yelled at him again—then knifed him in the side.
The man fell against the door, his hands locked on the wheel
and his shoulders rigid. The deputy was coming towards
them, playing his light on the windshield.

Agnes broke for it. He hit the door, banging at the handle.
Doug scrambled the length of the truck and opened the back
door. The television set was blocking his way, and as he pushed
it aside he saw Agnes, already up the road and running hard.
As he watched, a circle of light sped after Agnes, found his
feet and rose over him. Two shots sounded. Very close.

Instinctively Doug tried to locate the gun, but his view was blocked by the body of the truck. He jumped free and turned right into the prowl car coming up on the other side. He stopped as suddenly as if he'd hit something, his hands coming to rest at his sides.

They had cuffs on him before he saw the dark bundle lying on the side of the road. Huey went up to it, and in his light Doug saw the legs in the pale blue pants, spread on the ground in a frozen step.

He sat handcuffed in the back of the prowl car for over an hour, and their eyes were always on him. The owner of the television truck wasn't badly hurt; his leather jacket had almost turned away the small knife. After giving Huey a stumbling preliminary account, he walked slowly to his truck and started back towards town. He never once looked over to where Agnes was lying.

Huey and Pete didn't have much to say to each other after they radioed in their report. Pete sat sideways in the front seat, one eye on Doug, and Huey took a canvas tarp out of the trunk compartment and threw it over Agnes. Then he leaned into the car, his elbows resting on the window frame.

He looked at Doug and said, "This is the same one we caught the other day. How many times do we have to catch these punks?"

Pete remarked grimly, "We won't have to catch that one out there again."

Huey shifted and gazed bleakly out to where the tarp made a light spot on the roadside gravel. He shook his head. "I can't figure out why he tried to run. What'd he have to run for?"

Pete didn't attempt an answer.

CHAPTER TWELVE

The first night back in jail killed the days he had been free just as if they'd never happened. They vanished in a blur of bright-colored scenes until it seemed as if he'd only stepped out of the tank for a few minutes to have a strange dream of love and hatred, fear—and, finally, death. Later the days after the escape would expand again, taking on a higher color and clarity, and he would examine every turning like a general brooding over a lost battle.

When the doors banged in the morning, and he heard the rattle of the chow cart, he opened his eyes and saw the bunk mattress above him shift.

"Doug! What the hell?"

He winced. This is where he'd let Billy crawl to. But there was no knowledge of this in Billy's face, only an almost absurd eagerness. He looked paler, thinner, and his hair was sticking out from the sides of his head.

Billy jumped down and sat on the edge of Doug's bunk. "What happened? Where's Ernie?"

"The wheels came off."

"How'd they catch you?"

"Out on the road. They were waiting for us, just like they knew we were coming."

"Last night?"

"That's right. Early last night."

Billy looked puzzled. "I wouldn't have thought they'd sit out there that long. They get Ernie too?"

"No—"

"He got away?"

"Yes."

"Damn! Ain't that Ernie something? He's the luckiest bastard I know. How'd it happen?"

Billy was going to want to know everything. Doug didn't want to lie to him, but he didn't want to tell him the truth either. He stalled, looking around the cell. Armando was in the top bunk across from him, his face still closed in sleep. A man he didn't know was in the fourth bunk. Then he noticed that the door wasn't open and he asked why.

Billy told him, "Hell, we're lucky we're not in the Hole. We would be, but there's only room for one down there. We'll probably be locked up until they take us to the joint."

"Do you think we'll go there?"

"Are you kidding? We've got a lock on it. I don't know about you, but that's where I was going right along. And if you had any chance of beating it, you blew it when you cut out."

The future seemed to close around him again and he shivered a little in spite of himself. "What's it like?"

"I don't know. You can bet it's no summer camp. I never thought I'd be going up without Ernie. I guess he's long gone."

The door shuddered, and Billy jumped up and moved to the back of the cell. "Chow. You'd better stay away from the door."

A trusty appeared with a jailer right behind him. While the trusty pushed the bowls through a crack in the door, the jailer bent down and peered in at Doug.

"Well, another one home to the nest. Your buddy didn't have much sense, did he?"

Doug didn't try to answer, but he couldn't look away. The jailer nodded with a wise grimness.

"You know you're lucky the same thing didn't happen to you. You know that?" The door shot closed and he rattled it to see that it was tight. "You'd better wise up."

The jailer left. No one paid any attention to the food sitting on the floor. Armando was still asleep. The other man was sitting up, stretching, his face creased with sleep. Doug remembered him as one of the men he'd seen before, but he didn't know him.

"Doug—"

He'd been waiting for Billy's voice. For a moment he went on picking at the knee of his pants, then he turned. Billy was standing in front of the wash basin. His face seemed stiff.

"Billy, I lied to you. Ernie's dead. They—"

"Don't put me on!"

"Believe me. He's dead. They shot him last night when he tried to get away." He told Billy just how it happened, and Billy didn't move at all until he'd finished, then he kicked fiercely at nothing and turned his face to the wall.

"What'd they have to kill Ernie for? What the hell did he ever do to deserve that?"

Doug didn't know who Billy was asking, but he knew it wasn't himself.

The other man spoke, clearing his throat heavily. "He ran. Just like he done the other night. You can't always outrun bullets."

"Shut up!" Billy still didn't turn around.

"I don't think they were very happy about it," Doug said. "They kept me out there until the ambulance came. I heard them talking. I don't think they like it happening like that."

"Hell with what they liked. That don't help Ernie."

Billy climbed into his bunk and it was obvious that he didn't want to talk any more. Doug became aware of someone watching him and turned to see Armando's eyes above his blankets. Then Armando turned his face to the wall. The other man ate some of the mush, but poured most of it in the toilet. He tapped Doug's bowl.

"You want this stuff?"

"Just the bread."

"You better save something. They skip us at lunch. Not that it matters much." Then he laughed, but without humor, a weary wheezing. "That kid gets shot, and all that happens to us is that we have to go without lunch. If there's any sense to it, I can't see it."

CHAPTER THIRTEEN

Terrel called him out in the middle of the morning. Johnson wasn't with him this time—another man was waiting for them in the booking room, an older man with a head that seemed too large for his features. He wore a belted hunting coat and a big white stetson. Doug recognized him. It was the cop that had sent him to the mission his first night in town.

They cuffed him and watched him closely until they were inside the room they used for questioning. Terrel had another deputy lock the door behind them, then he walked around the table and dropped his briefcase on it. The older cop strolled over and looked out the window; his hands were clasped behind him and a plume of cigar smoke wove up his back.

They hadn't said anything to him and it was beginning to make him nervous. He stood in back of a chair—it never entered his mind to sit down.

Terrel leaned his knuckles on the table and stared at him. "Just what the hell did you think you were up to?"

"I don't know."

"You don't know?" Terrel snapped back in disgust. "Do you know you could have been shot, too? Do you know that?"

"Yes, sir."

Terrel rapped once with his knuckles and sat down. He indicated that Doug should sit and then he opened his brief case, but he didn't take anything out of it. "That buddy of yours was quite a boy. Do you know he almost killed a man in his own state?"

"No, sir. I didn't know much of anything about him."

The older man turned around and spoke softly. "Then why'd you let him talk you into escaping with him?"

Doug saw his eyes move above the cigar and they were mild, an old quiet blue like a faded work shirt.

"I don't know...." Doug tried to answer, but there was so much he didn't know how to say. "I just wanted to go, I guess."

"Christ!" Terrel exclaimed, shaking his head in real agitation. "Don't you kids ever think at all? Don't you ever consider consequences? There's one boy dead already, and God knows what else—all on an escape where you were beat before you really started. Do you know how little chance you had? How do you think we were waiting out there for you?" Terrel paused and started at him angrily. "Because the very man who sold you those hacksaws came and told us you had them."

The older man came over and sat on the edge of the table. "Kids don't always think like that, Bob. They wise up after awhile."

"It's a little late for this one."

"Maybe not."

Doug felt the mild eyes on him and he looked up into them.

"You should have tried the mission, boy. Did they arrest you that night?"

"Yes, sir."

He turned to Terrel. "Those other charges are out, Bob. I saw this kid climb off the bus. Now—you feel like telling us what happened the last couple of days?"

He didn't know how to start. What had they done besides run and hide?

Terrel broke into his thoughts. "Start with that first night. We know about the cleaners. You left your jacket on the roof."

"I know I did." It seemed to take something from the accusation that it didn't surprise him.

"What'd you go in there for?"

"I don't know. Money, I guess—"

"Money? You took that suit you got on, didn't you?"

He looked down at the suit, wrinkled and dirty now. He'd forgotten it wasn't his.

"Don't bother to lie," Terrel said. "It's on the report as missing, and that—"

The older man interrupted, patting his hand lightly on the table. "That ain't too important right now, Bob. We want that other fellow. Is he still hiding out in the same place?"

"Hiding out?"

"That's right. Who were you staying with?"

"We weren't with anyone. We just hid around."

"Around where?" Terrel demanded.

"Down by the tracks—"

"Nuts!" Terrel looked disgusted. "We *know* you were hiding out with someone. And this guy Pesco's still there."

Pesco?

"We never saw Pesco. I didn't even know him."

"But you *were* hiding out with some girls, weren't you?"

He thought of Marion and shook his head firmly. "There wasn't anyone. Honest."

The older man took his hat off and ran his hand over his crushed hair. When he spoke his voice had taken on a little more weight.

"Boy, you any idea how much trouble you're in? You know what kidnapping is?"

Automatically he said, "Yes, sir," but he didn't have any idea what he meant by it, except he knew, in a different sense, that he'd lost his life almost as much as Ernie had, and he felt regret for the man he thought he might have been.

Terrel was saying something, explaining about a call from some girl who hadn't given her name. Bet. She'd put those deputies out on the road. He saw Bet as they'd left her, sitting on the floor, with the mark of Ernie's hand wrapped around her face. She'd slapped back a hundred times harder.

"Look, boy, I'm Chief of Deputies, and I'm not up here talking to you because of that cleaners you busted into or that furniture store either. That was you too, wasn't it? Never mind. All that ain't too important now. But this Pesco is. We want him."

The chief paused and ran his finger along his lower lip, studying Doug as if he was sure Doug understood and wanted to do the right thing if he were only told what it was.

"Now you tell us where Pesco's holed up. We know it's with this same girl. Then when the time comes to charge you maybe it don't have to be kidnapping. You understand? You don't owe these people anything. Pesco's a killer, and a girl like this one can't be much good. There's no sense in you sheltering them with your own life."

They waited in silence, both of them following his face, while he thought, If it was just Bet I could send them and let them see how wrong they are.

"What's her name?" Terrel asked.

He was on the verge of telling them the truth, that they'd never seen Pesco, and that the girls didn't know where they were from—but he realized that if he even admitted the girls existed at all, these two men would pull everything out of him. He didn't feel anything towards Bet or Jinx, but he couldn't give them Marion. He could sell himself, but not her.

"We never talked to anyone the whole time, except some girls in the show. And we didn't see Pesco. I didn't even know that he'd got away."

He continued to shake his head for another half hour. Terrel got angry, but the old man just battered at him with his kindness, which was much harder to resist than Bailey Johnson's hands. Finally the old man sighed, stretched, and put his hat back on.

"Looks like we're waiting out time, Bob." His eyes rested for a moment on Doug's face. "I guess I misjudged you, young fellow. Looks like you're one of those who's got to have it the hard way. Lock him up."

Terrel nodded. "I'm going to get this suit back."

Terrel had him take the suit off in the booking room, unlocking the cuffs so he could get the coat off, and putting them back on before allowing him to take the pants off. He sat on a bench in his shorts while a deputy on the desk went to find him some coveralls.

He realized he was shivering, but he knew it wasn't from cold. His old man would help him, would have to help him whether he wanted to or not, but even as he clutched at the idea, he knew he'd never ask him, never let him know. He'd made this mess by wanting to be on his own—so now he was on his own.

He found he was covering himself with his arms and he tried to relax. It wasn't that he felt foolish in his underwear, or even ashamed of being uncovered while others were dressed—

But he was ashamed that even the clothes he'd been wearing belonged to somebody else, and like fairy gold they'd fallen away, leaving him without a single thing he could call his own. Except himself.

THE END